PUFFIN BOOKS

STORIES FOR CHRISTMAS
Alison Uttley

Chosen by Kathleen Lines

Christmas is a time of year with a special magic and enchantment all of its own, especially when celebrated in the traditional country way that Alison Uttley knew and loved when she was a child: blazing log fires, mince pies, red holly berries and the peal of church bells ringing out over snow-covered fields. Her stories capture the warmth and fun of Christmas when everybody and everything joins in the celebrations, from the trees and the birds of the forest to the lovable Sam Pig and his friends.

From the great treasure trove of Alison Uttley's work, Kathleen Lines has selected twelve Christmas stories. The result is a charming anthology that will help to bring the magic of Christmas alive for all five- to eight-year-olds.

Fairy Tales, another anthology of Alison Uttley's stories chosen by Kathleen Lines, is also available in Young Puffins.

ALISON UTTLEY

STORIES FOR CHRISTMAS

Chosen by Kathleen Lines

Illustrated by Gavin Rowe

PUFFIN BOOKS

in association with Faber & Faber

Puffin Books, Penguin Books Ltd, Harmondsworth, Middlesex, England
Penguin Books, 625 Madison Avenue, New York, New York 10022, U.S.A.
Penguin Books Australia Ltd, Ringwood, Victoria, Australia
Penguin Books Canada Ltd, 2801 John Street, Markham, Ontario, Canada L3R 1B4
Penguin Books (N.Z.) Ltd, 182–190 Wairau Road, Auckland 10, New Zealand

—

First published by Faber & Faber Ltd 1977
Published in Puffin Books 1981
Reprinted 1982

—

—

Filmset, printed and bound in Great Britain by
Hazell Watson & Viney Ltd, Aylesbury, Bucks
Set in VIP Bembo

CONTENTS

CONTENTS

FOREWORD

Christmas was the climax of winter for the country people during Alison Uttley's childhood. Ribbon and ornaments were carefully kept from year to year, holly and ivy and other greenery were gathered in the woods for decoration; few presents were bought, for most were handmade, and the traditional Christmas food was cooked or made at home. It is natural then that many of Alison Uttley's stories should be about the festival and the preparations for it. Many of them begin on Christmas Eve, 'that night of mystery when strange things can happen', the night that Santa Claus leaves the far north in a sleigh piled high with presents, drawn by nimble-footed reindeer, to visit the children of earth, and the wild creatures too; the night when fairies fly abroad as well as angels, when there is magic entwined in mystery, when visions may be seen in church, lonely cottage or dark forest; the night when all creation is united in the joy of the Nativity. And this joy is everywhere – beside the cottage fire, in field and wood, and in the heart of snow itself – the kingdom of Jack Frost.

Here are twelve stories of magic, enchantment and mystery, including two about Sam Pig (slightly edited to avoid confusing references to other Sam Pig stories which do not appear in this selection). These *Stories for Christmas* have been chosen from eight books written and published over many years, and they demonstrate Alison Uttley's long-lasting creativity, her sustained invention and the unique quality of her imagination.

KATHLEEN LINES

The Little Fir-Tree

It was a few days before Christmas, and the Old Grey Woman, who lives in the sky, was busy plucking her geese. The mighty birds lay across her broad knees, and she pulled out the white feathers and scattered them on the earth below.

'Pouf! Away they go! What a litter they make to be sure!' she sighed, and her voice was like the wind howling and moaning far away. Through the air the feathers delicately fluttered, tumbling, tossing, whirling in eddies, and the children looked through their windows and shouted gleefully: 'It's snowing! Look! Snow for Christmas!' and they jumped for joy.

'I told you so,' said their mother. 'I said it would snow. The sky was grey and heavy with the Old Woman up there.'

'Tomorrow we'll play snowballs, and ride in the sledge and make a snowman,' cried the children excitedly, as they went to bed.

Soon the earth was white, covered with the fine feathery mantle thrown down from the sky. The grass and trees felt warm under the snow. In the wood every dark branch was outlined with silver, and every holly leaf held a bunch of snowflakes in its hollowed green cup. The great beeches spread out their bare boughs and caught the snow in the net of twigs, and the birches stood like frozen fountains, very beautiful.

Near the edge of the wood was a plantation of fir-trees all very young and small. Their dark outstretched skirts were soon white, so that each tree looked like a little shining umbrella. Now one tree was different from the others, for it possessed a treasure which it held tightly to its heart. It was a nest, which had been built in the spring by a speckled thrush. It was so neat and trim that the fir-tree was very proud of it, and sheltered it with its close thick branches so that no snow fell into it.

The little fir-tree had loved the singing bird which lived there. It had taken care of the eggs and guarded the nestlings from owls and robbers till they were old enough to fly away. It had listened to the thrush's song, and moved its slender branches to the music. When the birds went, the tree waited for them to return or for another bird to come to the empty nest, but the rain fell, and the winds blew, and no bird sat in the home hidden in the heart of the tree.

'Perhaps a winter bird will come, a dazzling white bird, and it will lay eggs of ivory and pearl in my nest,' said the little fir-tree when it saw the snow, but the other trees round it shook their heads till the snow fell in a shower.

'Only hens could do that,' said they, 'and they stay in the farmyards this wintry weather. There will be no bird till next year.'

Then they drooped their branches and waited patiently till they were completely covered up again by the warm white blanket.

In a cottage down the lane lived a little boy and girl. They made a fine snowman outside their kitchen window, and stuck an old broken pipe of their grandfather's in its wide mouth, and a stick in its hand. They pulled each other up and down the fields in a wooden box, pretending it was a sledge drawn by a pair of fine horses. They made a long slide in the lane, and glided along it, with arms outstretched to the cold air, pretending they were flying birds. They looked at the icy frost-ferns on the windows of the little rooms under the thatched roof, and called them 'Jack Frost's Garden'.

'The children at the castle are going to have a Christmas tree,' proclaimed Peter, pushing his wet red hand into his mother's.

'And it's going to be all a-dazzle with lights and things,' said Sarah.

'Such things are not for us. They cost too much money, but you are going to have a pair of boots apiece, and that's more useful. Maybe Santa Claus will put something in your stocking, too, if you've been good.' Their mother sighed, knowing how hard it was to manage. She packed them off early to bed, but the grandfather nodded his head and smiled to himself.

On Christmas Eve the old man came into the wood, carrying a spade. He hunted here and there looking at this tree and that, peering at the colony of firs like a wise owl that wants to find a home. One tree was too big, another too scraggy, another too bushy. Then he saw the little fir-tree, standing like a fairy on one leg, wearing a crinoline of snowy crystals.

'That's the tree! That's the tree for me! Not too big, and not too little, with plenty of close branches, as smooth and round as a bell,' he cried aloud, for like many old people he had a habit of speaking to himself for company.

He shook the snow from the twigs with tender old fingers and then dug round the tree, gathering all the fibrous roots carefully in his hands.

'Oh dear me!' cried the little fir-tree. 'What is going to happen? Do be careful, old man. Don't shake the nest out of my branches!' The sound of its voice was like a sobbing breeze, and the other trees shook their heads and waved their tiny boughs mournfully.

'Good-bye,' they called. 'Good-bye for ever.'

'Whatever happens, I am glad. It's a great adventure,' the little fir-tree sang out bravely, when the old man carried it away.

Across the fields and along the lane it went in the grandfather's warm hands, and the tall trees in the hedgerows looked with pity at it. Little rabbits peeped round the corners of the walls, and a hare stared through a gap to see who was singing the song of the woods. When they saw the fir-tree they nodded and whispered: 'Poor thing! He's caught in a trap!' and they scurried away.

The grandfather walked through a wooden gate, and up the garden path to the cottage door. Then he put the tree in the wood-shed till the children went to bed. He wiped his spade, washed his hands and sat down to tea without saying anything.

At last it was bedtime, and Peter and Sarah had their baths on the kitchen hearth, where a great fire blazed, and sparks flew up the chimney. They sat on their stools and ate their bread and milk, and a mince-pie because it was Christmas Eve. Then they each took a candle and trundled up the crooked stair to their little beds, but just as they kissed good night to their mother and grandfather, Peter lifted his head and listened.

'I can hear a little singing noise,' said he. 'What is it?'

Sarah listened too. 'It's only the wind in the wood-shed,' she told her brother, and she ran to tie her stocking to the bedpost, ready for Santa Claus.

When all was quiet upstairs, the grandfather fetched the little tree into the house. The fire crackled, and the tree began to tremble with the heat, so that the twigs rustled and its song died away with fright. 'This is the end,' it thought.

'Here's a little tiddly Christmas tree for Peter and Sarah,' said the old man. 'But take great care of it, for I must put it back in the wood where I found it.'

The mother dropped her sewing and smiled at her father.

'Oh, Grandfather! What a surprise! What a perfect little tree!'

She gazed at the green tree, with its shining branches, to which a powder of snow still clung. There was something particularly beautiful about this tree, fresh from its dreams in the wood. As for the little fir-tree, it plucked up its courage and stared round the room, at the table with the bread and cheese, and the cat on the hearth, and the china dogs on the mantelpiece, and the holly wreath over the loud-ticking clock.

'There's a nest in it,' went on the grandfather, proudly. 'Peter will like that,' and he showed the mother the neat round nest hidden under the branches.

'Now I'm going out to buy some things to hang on it, so that it will be as fine as the tree up at the castle. You plant it carefully all ready for me!' He reached up to the teapot on the mantelpiece, the lustre teapot which was his money-box, and took out some coins.

'I'm going to be extravagant for once, for I've got a bit of my pension left,' he laughed, and he set off down the dark lanes to the village shop.

While he was away, the mother planted the tree in plenty of soil in the big earthenware breadmug which stood in the corner of the room, stocked with her home-made loaves. The bread she placed in a row on the dresser, small round cobs, each with a cross on the top in memory of the Christ Child, and the tree she dragged to the middle of the room, near the lamp and her sewing. As her needle went in and out she heard a tiny singing sound, and she knew it was the happy tree chanting its woodland song.

After some time the old man came back with a brown-paper parcel and bulging pockets. From the parcel he took little red and blue and gold balls to hang on the tree, and a silver glass trumpet, and four tiny coloured glass bells with little clappers which tinkled like icicles. He had a box of silver tinsel tassels to droop from the boughs like falling water, and a couple of golden roses. He brought from his pockets two oranges, and three rosy apples, and a couple of tiny baskets of almond fruits. The mother and the old man hung them all about the tree, so that it looked as if the little glossy fir-tree had stepped straight out of fairyland.

On the tip-top of the tree's head, the grandfather's shaking fingers fastened a little Dutch doll with a wisp of tinsel round her waist, a midget of a doll as big as his thumbnail, and in the nest he placed a lovely glass bird, with a white body and feathery tail and a silver beak and wings.

The tree quivered with delight, so that all the bells began to ring, and all the balls and sparkles jumped up and down and gleamed in the firelight. At last a bird had come to live in the nest again, a winter bird, snow-white like the frosty earth!

Throughout Christmas Eve the tree stayed in the quiet room, listening to the ticking of the clock, and the chink, chink of the dying fire, and the chirrup of the cricket which lived under the hearthstone, and the tree, too, murmured and rustled its branches, waiting for the glass bird to chirp and sing.

Then dawn came, and the mother made the fire again, so that the lights sprang out and the tree's dark branches reflected the glow. The kettle sang, the blue cups and saucers were placed with their tinkling spoons on the clean white cloth, and the bacon hissed in the frying-pan.

Suddenly there was a patter of feet, and a sound of laughter on the stairs. The door burst open and the two children came running in, carrying bulging little stockings in their hands.

'A Merry Christmas! A Merry Christmas!' they cried, hugging their mother and grandfather. Then they saw the pretty tree standing as demure as a little girl in her first party frock, and they gave a shout.

'A Christmas tree! Where did it come from? Oh! How lovely! It's a real live one, growing.'

'There's a teeny, tiny doll on the top. Is it for me?' asked Sarah.

'There's a real nest,' exclaimed Peter, 'and there's a bird in it, too.' They both danced round the tree singing:

> Christmas comes but once a year,
> And when it comes it brings good cheer.

'Just see if that bird has laid any eggs,' said the smiling old grandfather, and when Peter slipped his hand in the thrush's nest he found two silver sixpences!

That was a day for the fir-tree to remember. Never as long as it lived would it forget that day! It stood, the centre of the festivities, watching the Christmas games, listening to the Christmas songs, humming softly to the bells from the church across the village green.

'Can't you hear it?' whispered Peter. 'The tree is singing.' But Sarah said it was only the wind through the keyhole, for trees never sang.

In a few days the grandfather took the fir-tree back to the wood, with the nest safe and sound under the branches. He uncovered the hole, and planted the roots deep in it, so that the tree stood firmly among its companions.

'Tell us again,' cried the fir-trees in the plantation, when the little tree had told its story for the hundredth time. 'Did you say a snow-white bird came to live in your nest? Did you have bells on your boughs? And gold roses? Tell us again.'

So once more the fir-tree told the story of Christmas.

'But the bird never sang at all,' it added. 'I shall be glad to see my thrush again next spring. The bells were not as sweet-sounding as the bluebells in the wood, and the roses had no scent at all. But it was a beautiful Christmas, and I was very, very happy!'

The Christmas Box

In a small thatched cottage near the edge of the forest lived four young pigs – Tom, Bill, Ann and Sam, and with them, for much of the year, was their guardian Brock the Badger. The little pigs loved dear, kind Brock, and they looked up to him because of his strength and courage and because of his great wisdom.

Winter had come early. By December the pond was frozen solid and the snow lay deep. Every morning when he awoke Sam Pig thought about Christmas Day. He looked at the snow, and he shivered a little as he pulled on his little trousers and ran downstairs. But the kitchen was warm and bright and a big fire burned in the hearth. Tom cooked the porridge and Ann set the table with spoons and plates, and Bill ran out to sweep the path or to find a log for the fire.

After breakfast Sam fed the birds. They came flying down from the woods, hundreds of them, fluttering and crying and stamping their tiny feet, and flapping their slender wings. The big birds – the green woodpeckers, the blue-spangled jays, the dusky rooks and the speckled thrushes – ate

from large earthen dishes and stone troughs which Sam filled with scraps. They were always so hungry that the little birds got no chance, so Sam had a special breakfast table for robins and tom tits, for wrens and chaffinches. On a long flat stone were ranged rows of little polished bowls filled with crumbs and savouries. The bowls were walnut-shells, and every bird had its own tiny brown nutshell. Sam got the shells from the big walnut-tree in the corner of the farmer's croft. When autumn came the nuts fell to the ground, and Sam carried them home in a sack. The walnuts were made into nut-meal, but the shells were kept for the smallest birds.

After the bird-feeding Sam went out on his sledge. Sometimes Bill and Tom and Ann rode with him. Badger had made the sledge, but he never rode on it himself. He was too old and dignified, but he enjoyed watching the four pigs career down the field and roll in a heap at the bottom.

'Good old Badger,' thought Sam. 'I will give him a nice Christmas present this year. I'll make him something to take back to his house in the woods when he goes for his winter sleep.'

Badger of course never retired before Christmas, but when the festival was over he disappeared for three months and left the little family alone.

That was as far as Sam got. Ann was busy knitting a muffler for Badger. It was made of black

and white sheep's wool, striped to match Badger's
striped head. Bill the gardener was tending a blue
hyacinth which he kept hidden in the wood-shed.
Tom the cook had made a cake for Brock. It was
stuffed with currants and cherries and almonds as
well as many other things like honey-comb and
ants' eggs. Only young Sam had nothing at all.

There was plenty of time to make a present, he
told himself carelessly, and he swept up the snow
from the path and collected the small birds'
walnut-shells.

'Christmas is coming,' said a robin brightly.
'Have you got your Christmas cards ready, Sam?'

'Christmas cards?' said Sam. 'What's that?'

'You don't know what a Christmas card is?
Why, I'm part of a Christmas card! You won't
have a good Christmas without a few cards,
Sam.'

Sam went back to the house where Ann sat by
the fire knitting Badger's muffler. She used a pair
of holly-wood knitting needles which Sam had
made. A pile of scarlet holly-berries lay in a bowl
by her side and she knitted a berry into the wool
for ornament here and there. The blackthorn
knitting needles with their little white flowers
were, of course, put away for the winter. She only
used those to knit spring garments.

Sam sat down by her side and took up the ball of
wool. He rubbed it on his cheek and hesitated, but
Ann went on knitting. She wondered what he was
going to say.

'Ann. Can I make a Christmas card for Badger?' he asked.

Ann pondered this for a time, and her little needles clicked in tune with her thoughts.

'Yes, I think you can,' said she at last. 'I had forgotten what a Christmas card was like. Now I remember. There is a paintbox in the kitchen drawer, very, very old. It belonged to our grandmother. She used to collect colours from the flowers and she kept them in a box. Go and look for it, Sam.'

Sam went to the drawer and turned over the odd collection of things. There were cough-lozenges and candle-ends, and bits of string, and a bunch of rusty keys, a piece of soap and a pencil, all stuck together with gum from the larch-trees. Then, at the back of the drawer, buried under dead leaves and dried moss he found the little paintbox.

'Here it is! Oh Ann! How exciting,' cried Sam, and he carried it to the table.

'It's very dry and the paints all look the same colour,' said Ann, 'but with a good wash they'll be all right.'

'It's a very nice box of paints,' said Sam, and he licked each paint carefully with his pointed tongue.

'They taste delicious,' said he, smacking his lips. 'The colours are all different underneath, and the tastes are like the colours. Look, Ann! Here's red, and here's green and here's blue, all underneath this browny colour.'

He held out the box of licked paints which were now gaily coloured.

'The red tastes of tomatoes and the green of wood-sorrel and the blue of forget-me-nots,' said Sam.

Badger was much interested in the paintbox when he came in.

'You will want a paint-brush,' said he. 'You can't use the besom-brush, or the scrubbing-brush, or even your tooth-brush to paint a Christmas card, Sam.'

'Nor can he use the Fox's brush,' teased Bill.

Badger plucked a few hairs from his tail and bound them together.

'Here! A badger-brush will be excellent, Sam.'

'What shall I have to paint on?' asked Sam, as he sucked the little brush to a point and rubbed it on one of the paints.

That puzzled everybody. There was no paper at all. They looked high and low, but it wasn't till Tom was cooking the supper that they found the right thing. Tom cracked some eggs and threw the shells in the corner. Sam took one up and used the badger-brush upon it.

'This is what I will have,' he cried, and indeed it was perfect, so smooth and delicate. Bill cut the edges neatly and Sam practised his painting upon it, making curves and flourishes.

'That isn't like a Christmas card,' said Ann, leaning over his shoulder. 'A Christmas card must have a robin on it.'

'You must ask the robin to come and be painted tomorrow,' said Brock. 'He will know all about it. Robins have been painted on Christmas cards for many years.'

After the birds' breakfast the next day Sam asked the robin to come and have a picture made.

'I will sit here on this holly branch,' said the robin. 'Here is the snow, and here's the holly. I can hold a sprig of mistletoe in my beak if you like.'

So Sam fetched his little stool and sat in the snow with his paintbox and the badger-brush, and the robin perched on the holly branch, with a mistletoe sprig in its beak. It puffed out its scarlet breast and stared with unwinking brown eyes at Sam, and he licked his brush and dipped it in the red and blue and green, giving the robin a blue feather and a green wing.

'More eggshells,' called Sam, and he painted so fast and so brightly that the robin took one look and flew away in disgust.

'That's a bird of Paradise,' said he crossly.

Sam took his eggshells indoors and hid them in a hole in the wall, ready for Christmas Day.

'Have you a Christmas present for Badger?' asked Ann. 'I have nearly finished my scarf, and Tom's cake is made, and Bill's hyacinth is in bud. What have you made, Sam?'

'Nothing except the Christmas card,' confessed Sam. 'I've been thinking and thinking, but I can't find anything. If I could knit a pair of stockings, or grow a cabbage, or make a pasty I should know what to give him, but I can't do nothing.'

'Anything,' corrected Ann.

'Nothing,' said Sam. 'I can only play my fiddle –'

'And fall in the river and steal a few apples, and get lost and catch the wind – ' laughed Ann. 'Never mind. You shall share my scarf if you like, Sam, for you helped to find the sheep's wool and you got the holly-berries for me.'

Sam shook his head. 'No. I won't share. I'll do something myself.'

He went out to the woods, trudging through the snow, looking for Christmas presents. In the holly-trees were scarlet clusters of berries, and the glossy ivy was adorned with black beads. The rest of the trees, except the yews and fir-trees, were bare, and they stood with boughs uplifted, and their trunks faintly smudged with snow. There wasn't a Christmas present anywhere. The willows, from which Badger had once made a boat, were smooth and ruddy, with never a parcel or packet or treasure among them. Then something waved in a thorn bush, something fluttered like a white flag, and Sam ran forward. The wind was rising and it made a curious moan and a whistle as it ruffled Sam's ears and made them ache. He stretched up to the little flag and found it was a feather. A feather! Sam had a thought! Perhaps the wind blew it to him, but there it was, a feather!

'I'll make him a feather bed, and when he goes to his castle deep in the woods he will take it with him to lie on. Poor old Badger, sleeping alone on the hard ground. Yes, I'll make him a feather bed.'

When the birds came for their breakfast the next morning Sam spoke to them about it.

'Can you spare a feather or two? I want to make a feather bed for old Badger's Christmas present,' he told them.

The birds shook their wings and dropped each a loose feather; they brushed and combed themselves and tossed little feathers to the ground. They passed the word round among the tree families, and other birds came flying with little feathers in their beaks for Sam Pig. A flock of starlings left a heap of glistening shot-silk, and the rooks came cawing from the bare elms with sleek black quills. The chattering magpies brought their black and white feathers, which Sam thought were like Badger's head. The jays came with their bright blue jewels, and the robins with scarlet wisps from their breasts. A crowd of tits gave him their own soft little many-coloured feathers, and even the wood pigeons left grey feathers for Sam. He had so many the air was clouded with feathers so that it seemed to be snowing again. He gathered them up and filled his sack, and even then he had some over. He put the beautiful tiny feathers in his pocket, the red scraps from the robins, the blue petals of feathers from the tits, the yellow atoms from the goldfinches and the emerald-blue gems from the kingfisher. These he wove into a basket as small as a nutshell, for Sister Ann, and inside he put some mistletoe pearls. Ann would like this, he knew.

On Christmas Day Sam came downstairs to the kitchen, calling 'A merry Christmas' to everybody. He didn't hang up his stocking of course because he had no stockings, and he didn't expect any presents either. Badger was the one who got the presents, old Badger who was the friend and guardian of the four pigs. It was at Christmas time they made their gifts to thank him for his care. So all the little pigs came hurrying downstairs with their presents for him.

There stood Badger, waiting for them, with a twinkle in his eye. Ann gave him the black and white muffler with its little scarlet berries interwoven.

'Here's a muffler for cold days in the forest, Brock,' said she.

'Just the thing for nights when I go hunting,' said Brock, nodding his head and wrapping the muffler round his neck.

Then Bill gave him the little blue hyacinth growing in a pot.

'Here's a flower for you, Brock, which I've reared myself.'

'Thank you, Bill. It's the flower I love,' said Brock and he sniffed the sweet scent.

Then Tom came forward with the cake, which

was prickly with almonds and seeds from many a plant.

'Here's a cake, Brock, and it has got so many things inside it, I've lost count of them, but there's honey-comb and eggs.'

'Ah! You know how I like a slice of cake,' cried Brock, taking the great round cake which was heavy as lead.

Then little Sam came, with the feather bed on his back. He had embroidered it with the letter B made of the black and white magpie feathers.

'For you to sleep on in your castle,' said he.

'Sam! Sam!' everybody cried. 'And you kept it secret! That's what you were doing every morning when the birds came for their breakfast! We thought there seemed to be a lot of feathers on the ground!'

Badger lay down on the little bed and pretended to snore. He was delighted with the warm comfortable present from little Sam Pig.

'Never mind the weather but sleep upon a feather,' said he. 'I shall sleep like a top through the fiercest gale when I lie on this little bed.'

They had breakfast, with a lashing of treacle on their porridge from the tin which Ann had kept for festivals. Then Sam hurried out to feed the birds and to thank them again for their share in Badger's Christmas. He carried a basket full of walnut-shells stuffed with scraps, and he found hosts of birds hopping about waiting for him.

But when he stepped into the garden he gave a

cry of surprise, for in the flower bed grew a strange little tree.

'Look! Look!' he called. 'Ann! Bill! Tom! Badger! Come and look! It wasn't growing there last night. Where has it come from? And look at the funny fruit hanging on it! What is it?'

They followed him out and stared in astonishment at the small fir-tree, all hung with pretty things. There were sugar pigs with pink noses and curly tails of string; and sugar watches with linked chains of white sugar, and chocolate mice. There were rosy apples and golden oranges, and among the sweet dainties were glittering icicles and hoarfrost crystals.

'Where has it come from? How did it grow here?' they asked, and they turned to Badger. 'Is it magic?' they asked. 'Will it disappear? Is it really real?'

'It's solid enough, for the tree has come from the woods, but the other things will disappear fast enough I warrant when you four get near them.'

'But where did you find such strange and lovely things?' persisted Ann, staring up with her little blue eyes. 'Where? Where? From fairyland, Badger?'

'I went to the Christmas fair in the town. I walked up to a market stall and bought them with a silver penny I had by me,' said Brock.

'But did nobody say anything to you?' asked Sam. 'How did you escape?'

'They were all so busy they didn't notice a little

brown man who walked among them. They didn't bother about me on Christmas Eve. Miracles happen on Christmas Eve, and perhaps I was one of them.'

Then Sam Pig brought the little feather basket and hung it among the icicles for his sister Ann. She was enchanted by it, and strung the mistletoe pearls round her neck.

'But where are your Christmas cards, Sam?' she asked suddenly. 'This is the time to give them.'

'I sat on them, Ann,' confessed Sam. 'I put them on a chair and sat down on them.'

'Crushed Christmas cards,' murmured Tom the cook. 'They will do very well to give an extra flavour to the soup. Those reds and blues and greens will make the soup taste extra good, I'm sure.'

It was true. The Christmas soup with the Christmas card flavour was the nicest anyone had ever tasted, and not a drop was left.

As for the Christmas tree, everybody shared it, for the birds flew down to its branches and sang a Christmas carol in thanks for their breakfasts, and Sam sat underneath and sang another carol in thanks for their feathers.

So it was a very happy Christmas all round.

The Doll's House

'Christmas Eve and a cold snowy night,' sang the wind, as it flew over the fields with its arms full of snow.

'Christmas Eve! Christmas Eve! Wake up!' it howled, and it sped to the house on the hill. All was in darkness there. Not a light glimmered from the windows with their tightly drawn curtains and barred shutters. The wind banged at the doors, but they were locked and bolted. It rattled the shutters and knocked with its thin bony fingers at the glass of bedroom casements. Round the house it ran, pushing and poking, shrieking down the chimneys and through the keyholes, to tell everyone that it was Christmas Eve.

Then, high up, in the gable under the roof, it found a small pointed window which was unlatched. It pushed, and the tiny slit of a window in that narrow gable flew open. Into the room rushed the wind. It tinkled the chiming glasses that hung from the ceiling like bells. It blew the soot in the chimney and it tossed a flurry of ice crystals on the carpet.

The room had once been the nursery, but the children were tired of their old toys, and seldom visited them. Now it was a kind of workroom, an attic, a storeroom, a deserted place. In the alcove by the narrow slit window stood a doll's house. There it was, four-square, old-fashioned, stiff and dusty – a forgotten toy. Nobody ever came to see the little family that lived within. Nobody cared any longer.

The wind whistled down the red chimney into the tiny rooms. It puffed at the little green door with the brass knocker, and blew it open.

The dolls lay on the floor, where they had been thrown long ago: Highland Laddie, Fairy Doll, Lady Rose, Chimpy, Grannie and the Rag Doll. The wind blew over them, ruffled their hair and touched their cheeks with its fingers.

'Christmas Eve,' sang the wind, and its voice was sweeter and gentler in that forlorn place. 'Christmas Eve,' it called, and then away it went, through the tiny green door of the doll's house, through the narrow window of the old nursery, away across the countryside.

The dolls stirred in their long sleep. New life came into them from that magical touch of the wind, and they awoke.

'Did you hear something?' asked the little Highland Laddie, shaking his torn kilt and struggling to his feet. 'Did you hear what the wind said? It's Christmas Eve and – we've been forgotten.'

'Christmas Eve? What does that mean? I've been asleep so long I feel like Rip Van Winkle. I've forgotten everything.'

It was Lady Rose who spoke. She tossed her curls and straightened her flimsy silk dress. She drew the folds over a rent, and sighed over the shabbiness of her clothes. She had once been a famous beauty, but now she was old and worn.

'Christmas Eve?' cried Fairy Doll, and she sprang up and stood on one leg and spun round like a humming-top. 'I am a Fairy Doll. I was dressed in a silver-spangled frock, four, no – five years ago. I stood high on top of a Christmas tree with a silver wand in my hand and a star in my hair. Yes, I did!'

'We can't believe that tale,' said Lady Rose, coldly. 'We have heard it before. You, in your old rags and wisps of torn ribbon, could never have been a fairy on a tree. You've imagined it, because your name is Fairy Doll.'

'It *is* true,' protested the little Fairy Doll. 'I remember it. I remember the feeling of it all. I was so happy that night. Everybody looked at me, high up on top of that beautiful Christmas tree.'

'What's a Christmas tree?' asked a small voice, and the Rag Doll came out from a dark corner of the doll's house. She was indeed a little ragamuffin!

'Christmas! Christmas! Christmas!' chanted the woolly monkey, Chimpy, and he curled himself in a ball and rocked to and fro watching the others with his beady gold eyes.

All this time one doll remained silent. Her black eyes gazed benignly around, her red cheeks glowed with country health, her dark painted head had never a hair awry. She was dressed in a lavender print frock, with a very full gathered skirt, over a couple of white petticoats, scalloped with silk stitching round the bottom. On her round wooden head she wore a sunbonnet which framed her sturdy face to perfection. Her legs stuck stiffly out, so that her buttoned boots were against the table. Her jointed arms were folded on her frilled bodice, under a three-cornered shawl. She looked brave and independent. Her name was Grannie, for she was very old. She had belonged to the children's grandmother, and each generation had played with her and laughed at her. She was so old-fashioned, this Dutch doll, that they said she must have come out of the Ark.

She didn't care what anybody said, and now she sat in her corner, beaming at all of them, at the Highland Laddie in his ragged kilt, at Lady Rose in her faded silk, at the Fairy Doll in her tatters, and the Rag Doll, wrapped in a duster.

The snowflakes came whirling in at the nursery window, spinning down through the little green door of the doll's house, settling on the floor of the dolls' room. They smothered the

small table, and heaped themselves on the fireplace.

'Dear me!' murmured Lady Rose, shivering. 'I've never seen this before.'

'Nor I,' said the Rag Doll, trembling with fear.

'I'm used to it,' said Highland Laddie, proudly. 'I come from Edinburgh, and I remember this outside the shop window where I stood before somebody bought me and carried me here.'

'I remember it too,' whispered the Fairy Doll. 'I saw it when I was on top of the Christmas tree.'

'Nonsense,' snapped Lady Rose, but the Rag Doll began to weep, sobbing quietly to itself.

Then Grannie stood up. She hobbled across the little floor and wrapped the Rag Doll in her shawl.

'Hush, my child,' she whispered. 'It's Christmas Eve. You must not cry.'

'Grannie. Tell us about Christmas Eve,' pleaded the Fairy Doll. 'We have forgotten. Tell us about the snow and stars and everything.'

The ancient doll walked across the room to the little green door and peered out.

'Later,' said she. 'Now come with me. On this day we have the power. Follow me, and I'll show you.'

She nodded her little wooden head till her

bonnet strings came untied, and she beckoned to them all.

They ran after her into the nursery, where the snow now lay in a heap under the narrow window of the alcove. They waded through the drifts, kicking up the crystals, stamping their tiny feet, and admiring their footprints. They gathered up handfuls of snow, and made snowballs, the size of marbles. Even Lady Rose forgot her dignity and threw a snowball at Highland Laddie. As for Chimpy, the monkey, he was beside himself with joy, as he leapt about, eating the snow, rolling in it, till he was like a white monkey from Tibet.

Then Grannie took Chimpy aside, and whispered to him. She pointed with her wooden hand to the window through which they could see the topmost crest of the great fir-tree on the lawn. He nodded, and kicked his fluffy legs and turned a somersault. Away he went, up to the windowsill, where he balanced for a moment. Then, swinging by one brown arm, and taking a great leap, he dropped to the ground far below.

'Where has he gone? Is he lost? What's he going to do?' chattered the dolls, excitedly, but they could not climb to the window, and Grannie only smiled.

She got up on the nursery table and looked in the work-basket, for a reel of cotton, a pair of scissors, or anything she could find. Grannie dearly loved a work-basket, and she sat on the wicker edge, turning the little bone handle of the tape measure, stuffing her fist in the brass thimble, unwinding bits of coloured wool, and enjoying herself immensely.

'What are you doing, Grannie?' asked the Fairy Doll, peeping up at her.

Poor little Fairy Doll! She looked very ragged and worn against the silvery snow, and Grannie smiled down at her.

'Never you mind, my dear,' nodded Grannie. She snipped and snapped with the scissors, and stitched with a needle, and twisted the bright wools. She was very busy up there on top of the nursery table.

'You play with these, my dear,' she whispered, and she dropped a delicate pair of embroidery scissors to the Fairy Doll. 'See what you can make.'

The Fairy Doll held the fine scissors, which were so sharp they could cut a moonbeam into a thousand pieces. She found a piece of tissue paper, and she began to cut. Magical and wonderful things dropped from her fingers, as she ran the scissor points in and out. Lacy trees with apples in their boughs, a coach and six horses, dancing girls pirouetting on tiptoe, lakes with swans a-swimming and reeds round their edges, all these and more came out of the sheet of paper, as the Fairy Doll cut them.

Grannie glanced down at her and nodded again.

'Yes, even in a piece of paper, there are a thousand secrets hidden, if only we can discover them.'

Lady Rose was busy at the far end of the room. She had found the store cupboard, with a bag of flour, and a sack of sugar, and blue bags filled with currants and raisins. She tucked her faded silk dress round her waist, wrapped a duster about her for an apron, turned up her sleeves – and how she worked!

She carried pinches of this and that and mixed them in a little bowl with snow, which gave them a feathery lightness. She whisked them with an icicle, and beat them to a froth. She lighted the fire in the tin stove in the doll's house, and in a minute she was making cakes as fast as she could.

'I've never done this before,' she murmured complacently. 'I must be a born cook.'

She tasted with her little finger crooked in the dish, and then she popped the cakes into the tiny oven and shut the door. Soon there was a delicious smell that filled not only the doll's house but the nursery. The Fairy Doll sniffed hungrily, but she did not look up. Grannie smiled to herself, but she went on with her sewing. Highland Laddie licked his lips, and went on with his work too.

He was far away in the corner of the room,

content and happy. He had found a pocket knife with a sharp blade. He was carving something, away there by the stick-box. He snitched and cut the kindling wood, and made little toys of rare quality. There was a boat as big as a cobnut, a set of chairs that would go in a walnut, a pair of tiny clogs to fit Grannie's feet, and a necklace of carved wooden beads for Lady Rose.

As for the Rag Doll, she was painting with an old paintbox she had found. Nobody knew what she was making, but she dipped her brush in the snow, and dabbled it in scarlet and blue, as if she had painted all her life.

There was a scrabble at the window, and Chimpy fell into the room. He had been away so long the others had forgotten all about him.

'I've got it. I've got it, Grannie,' he shouted, capering across the room dragging the top of the fir-tree after him. He was smothered in snow, and when he shook himself and brushed the boughs of his green tree, the snow crystals flew in a flurry about the room, as if the snowstorm had come again.

'Clever Chimpy! That's our Christmas tree,' said Grannie. All the dolls left their work to stare at the lovely tree, so neatly shaped, so trim and compact.

The Grandmother doll came down from the table bearing a heap of beautiful things in her arms.

'Look what I've been making,' she said,

spreading out little roses, scarlet, pink, gold, which she had sewn from scraps of silk and wool. 'These are to decorate the Christmas tree.'

'And see what I've made,' cried the Fairy Doll. She danced round the room, tossing high in the air the paper ballet girls, her swans, her floating balls and her parasols, all cut in the most delicate manner from the thin tissue paper.

'I've made flags and streamers,' said the Rag Doll, holding up her painted strips and garlands, dazzling with colour.

Then Highland Laddie showed them the toys he had made, and the little Rag Doll clapped her hands with delight when he gave her a wooden purse with a cinder inside it.

'Where is Lady Rose?' asked everybody, but there was no need to look for her. Out of the doll's house chimney came a curl of blue smoke, and from the open green door came a most ravishing odour.

'I've been making the Christmas Eve supper,' said Lady Rose, popping her head round the corner, and brushing a hanging lock of hair from her face. She was grimy with soot and scarlet with heat, but she looked happier than she had ever done in all her life.

'The mince-pies will be ready in a few minutes now,' she smiled and disappeared.

'Quickly, everybody! Get the Christmas tree decorated,' commanded Grannie.

She set the little fir-tree in an empty bobbin, and put it on the floor of the doll's house.

She hung her coloured roses along the branches, as if they were growing in the greenery. The Highland Laddie placed his toys round the foot of the tree and hung his small presents, carefully wrapped in scraps of brown paper, on the boughs. The Rag Doll hung her streamers across the room, in gay array of many colours. The Fairy Doll pinned on the walls her cut-out swans and ballet girls, her coaches and six, and her lacy trees with apples in their branches.

Then Chimpy ran to the windowsill and returned with a bunch of sparkling icicles, which he hung on the tree, and frost crystals which he flung over the fir-needles, till they glittered and sparkled like fire.

'We must put a few stitches in ourselves,' said Grannie, and she took a needle from her bodice, to mend each doll's clothes. She stitched the rent in Highland Laddie's kilt, and sewed his sporran firmly on. She gathered up Lady Rose's torn dress, and she mended the Rag Doll's arm. Then, from under her full lavender skirt she drew a lovely silver frock for the Fairy Doll to wear, and a pair of silver wings as well. Nobody knew where she got them, for the material certainly wasn't in the work-basket, but old grandmother dolls have powers of their own on Christmas Eve.

'Thank you, oh, thank you, dear Grannie,' said the Fairy Doll, as she slipped the silver skirt over her head and dropped her rags. The Rag Doll fastened the wings to her shoulders and the Highland Laddie handed her a wand with a silver star on the end he had been keeping for her.

Fairy Doll danced round the room and out into the nursery, on tip-toe like a real ballet dancer. She swirled her short frilly skirt in a dazzling manner, and flew on her points like a bird. Back to the doll's house she went, and up the tree, where she balanced for a moment among the green branches, like the Fairy she was.

The Highland Laddie was enchanted, but Lady Rose banged the oven door.

'Supper's ready,' said she sharply. 'We've had enough dancing, thank you.' She wasn't at all pleased with the Fairy Doll's appearance.

'Cheers for Lady Rose,' interrupted old Grannie. 'She is a good cook, and cooks always get on well in the world.'

'Lady Rose. Three cheers,' echoed the others and they held up their little tawny wine glasses and drank her health in snow-wine.

What a merry supper that was! They ate and they drank, and the little candles gleamed in the doll's house candlesticks, and the tiny lamp glowed on the mantelpiece.

They sang carols with Grannie leading them in her thin old voice, and Highland Laddie played his bagpipes. Indeed, the skirl of the pipes came shrilly into the dreams of the children in the rooms below, and they turned in their sleep as they heard it.

Then Grannie took the little brown parcels from the Christmas tree and gave them away. Lady Rose had her necklace of carved wooden beads, and Rag Doll had a set of acorn buttons. Grannie put her wooden clogs on her feet, and said they were just what she wanted. Chimpy had a monkey-on-a-stick to play with. Then Fairy Doll unwrapped her parcel, and out fell a little wooden heart as big as a pea. It opened like a locket, and inside was a red curl from Highland Laddie's hair.

They all laughed and teased the Fairy Doll, but Lady Rose frowned.

'Not at all necessary,' said she. 'We all know that Highland Laddie loves the Fairy Doll without such sentimental nonsense.'

But nobody minded what Lady Rose said.

It was nearly midnight, and of course they knew that even Christmas Eve magic stops when the clock strikes twelve.

They sat round the fire, with Grannie in the middle. The trees shone in the candlelight, and the little roses seemed to be blooming there among the snow-crystals and icicles.

'On Christmas Eve,' said Grannie, 'I used to hear a piece of poetry. It was always the same. I believe I can remember a few lines even now.'

'Tell us, Grannie,' pleaded the Fairy Doll.

'Was it "Auld Lang Syne"?' asked the Highland Laddie. 'I heard them singing that at New Year.'

Grannie pursed her small red lips, and frowned a moment, and then she began, swaying backward and forward, and speaking in a low voice full of mystery.

'Twas the night before Christmas,
When all through the house,
Not a creature was stirring, not even a
  mouse.
The stockings were hung in the chimney with
  care,
In hopes that St Nicholas soon would be
  there.

'Why, that's it,' cried Grannie. 'I had forgotten. We must all hang up our stockings tonight. Santa Claus comes tonight, children. The great Saint Nicholas comes with gifts for all.'

'How does he come?' asked Highland Laddie.

'He drives in a sleigh drawn by eight tiny reindeer, of course,' cried Grannie, 'Listen. What's that?'

They all sat very still, and from across the lawn there came the sound of bells ringing. Nearer and nearer tinkled those little bells. The chime floated through the green door of the doll's house.

They rushed out, and clambered on a chair to look out of the window, high in the gable.

'Oh,' they cried. 'It *is* Saint Nicholas! Look at his red coat, and his white beard, and the eight tiny reindeer! Quick! Hang up your stockings and go to bed. He doesn't like to be seen.'

Grannie shooed them away, and they tore off their little black stockings and hung them on a string in front of the nursery fireplace. Then they went to bed.

Down below in the big house, the grandfather clock struck twelve. One Two Three – it tolled in its deep ancient voice. The dolls shut their eyes, they settled themselves on the floor of the doll's house. They were suddenly so tired they couldn't keep awake another second. The magic had worn off. They slept so soundly that they didn't even wake when somebody opened the nursery door.

'Hello, Jean. Look here,' cried a boy's voice. 'Look at these little queer stockings round the chimney. They weren't here when we were last in the nursery.'

Jean came tumbling into the room.

'What a strange thing!' she said. 'I've never seen such tiny stockings before. They are full too, packed to the brim with goodies and comfits.'

The children emptied the little stockings on to the table, and tasted the stars and moons made of sugar.

'Look at the snow on the floor,' said Jean.

'And all these footprints. Like a lot of birds – no – like tiny feet,' exclaimed John, stooping down to examine the pattern in the snow.

They opened the doll's house. On the floor lay the dolls and they lifted them out.

'See! They've got a Christmas tree of their own. Oh, look at the decorations, the roses and little toys, as big as pins!' cried John.

'Look at Fairy Doll's dress. Who can have done it? Who came up here in the night?' cried Jean. 'The Fairy Doll is pretty enough to go on our Christmas tree. I'll put her there.'

John was examining Highland Laddie.

'Somebody has stitched his kilt,' said he. 'I remember it was all torn. And Chimpy has a monkey-on-a-stick in his arms.'

'Grandmother must have done it,' they both agreed, and they ran downstairs with the dolls and little tree.

'You *must* have done it, Grandmother,' said Jean to the old lady in her corner by the fire. 'You must have gone upstairs to the nursery, and dressed the Fairy Doll and mended Highland Laddie.'

'And put a Christmas tree in the doll's house, and little toys there. You went upstairs to see your own old doll, Grandmother. Confess!' cried John shaking the tree so that the little icicles tinkled.

The Grandmother shook her head and held out her hand for the Grannie Doll.

'It must have been the Grannie Doll. She has powers at Christmas, they say. She always was an

49

original doll. Why, she is wearing a pair of wooden clogs. Where have they come from?'

The Grannie Doll smiled mysteriously at the Grandmother, and the old woman smiled back. They both knew a few secrets, those two, at Christmas time. They both knew how to hold their tongues on certain matters of magic.

But outside the wind blew over the fields, and its arms were filled with sunbeams.

'Christmas Day! Christmas Day!' it called, and the bells of the village church answered. The wind tossed the bands of sunlight down on the snowy pastures, so that they shone like rainbows come to earth. It puffed at the fir-tree, which had lost its top-knot, and it rattled at the windows of the house on the hill. Then it peeped through, at the great Christmas tree with the Fairy Doll on the top, and the tiny Christmas tree, with its wool roses and its icicles and unmelted frost crystals.

'Christmas Day and a fine frosty morning,' sang the wind, and it sped away to give the good news to all.

The Christmas Surprise

The clock struck eleven. The kitchen was empty, except for the cat sitting on the hearth, sleeping peacefully. The two children and their father were in bed.

'It's Christmas Eve. Why have you made no decorations? Why is nothing ready for Christmas Day?' asked a small indignant voice, as a mouse squeaked from under a chair.

'Oh, it's you,' muttered the cat, opening one eye. 'Don't you be too venturesome, even if it is Christmas Eve. No decorations indeed! Missis is ill, in hospital. Children can't do things alone. Mister is very sad.'

'*You* do something,' squeaked the mouse. 'It's Pax Night tonight, and we'll help you.'

'Pax? Peace? Yes, that's the law tonight. I won't eat you,' replied the cat. 'Go and get your friends and relations.'

The mouse ran off, and soon returned with a host of eager little helpers.

The cat stood up proudly and gave orders.

'Some of you go upstairs and fetch the

children's socks. They will be on the chairs by their beds,' she commanded.

Away scampered the mice, up the stairs, and soon came down dragging four socks. The cat hung the little socks on the clothes-line under the chimney. 'Now they are ready for the presents,' she said.

'What presents?' asked the mice.

'Santa Claus will come down the chimney and bring them presents, to fill their socks,' said the cat.

'Can we hang our stockings too?' asked the mice.

'If you like,' said the cat.

So the mice took off their furry stockings and hung them by the children's socks.

'What next?' asked the mice.

'Can you cook?' asked the cat.

'Yes, we are very good cooks,' said the mice. 'Toasted cheese, and fried bacon rinds.'

'No, Christmas fare. Can you make mince-pies?' The cat opened the larder door and put her paw into a jar of mincemeat. 'Here's flour and lard, to make pastry, and mincemeat to put in it, to make pies. Can you do it, or shall I?'

'Please will you do it, Mistress Cat?' squeaked the mice. So the cat put on a small apron which hung behind the door and measured out the flour and lard, using her paws.

She made fifty little mince-pies each as big as

a button, and she turned on the electric cooker and put them in the oven.

'Now for the cake,' said the cat.

'We'll make the cake,' cried the mice quickly. 'We know about cake-making and cake-eating.'

'Currants, raisins, sugar, butter, nuts – nice things to eat,' said one of the mice dreamily, and the rest ran to the larder and dragged out the bags of good things for the cake.

The cat broke the eggs and whisked them to a froth with her paw. The mice measured and mixed the cake with a lot of silver teaspoons, for the long wooden spoon was too heavy for them to lift. Then the cat gave a final swish as she dropped the beaten eggs in the mixture and the cake was put in a tin. The cat carried it to the oven and she lifted out the little mince-pies, crisp and delicious.

'While the cake cooks, we can get on with the decorations,' said the cat.

'I can make silver thread,' said a fat old spider who sat in her web. 'Shall I weave some shining threads round the room?'

She spun the long threads, swinging to and fro as she worked, and the beautiful web was drawn across the walls like a silver scarf.

'We will make little baubles to hang on it,' said the mice, and they nibbled some coloured papers which lay in the corner. They bit the papers into flowery shapes, so that there were pink roses, blue violets and purple and gold lilies, all cut and shaped by their little white teeth. The spider took these blossoms to her web and hung them from it to make a garland.

'We must have a Christmas tree and a kissing-bunch,' said the cat. 'I'll go to the wood for holly. All of you get on with the work while I am away. Mind the cake and don't let it burn.'

She leapt out of the window and ran to the woods, and the mice sighed with relief, and went on with their work of flower-making, taking a nibble now and then of the mince-pies.

They did not even hear the cat return with her load of holly berries, and her sprays of mistletoe, and the smallest fir-tree, only the size of the cat herself.

So with squeaks of delight they decorated the tree with their own small treasures, and scraps of ribbon, nibbled from a towel. They put the holly sprigs behind the dishes on the dresser, and over the saucepans and the pictures, and the grandfather clock.

'Sniff! Sniff!' went the cat. 'The cake is burning.'

She opened the oven door and took out the crisp sugary-sweet cake with its almonds on the top, and she put it on the prettiest plate she could find. A mouse placed a spray of holly in the middle and they all sat round admiring and smelling.

There was the sound of hoofs and little grunts of the reindeer outside. They all squeaked,

'Santa Claus is here.' There was a shuffle in the chimney and they all hid under the chairs, but the cat lay down serenely on the hearth.

Down the chimney came Santa Claus, with a bag on his back. He stepped over the smiling cat and looked around him.

'A Happy Christmas to all within this house,' said he quietly, and to his surprise there were little squeaky voices coming from every corner, little husky voices, excited and queer.

'A Happy Christmas to you, Santa Claus.'

'My goodness! Mice, lots of mice,' said Santa Claus, and he pulled his scarlet robe close to him. He filled the four socks with the nicest toys he could find, and then he sat down in the rocking-chair and sniffed at the cake and tasted a mince-pie.

'Now this kitchen is a real home for Santa Claus,' said he. 'I have never seen one quite so pretty as this in all my life. It must have been decorated by the fairies.'

'Miaow,' mewed the cat. 'Not fairies but mice.'

'Not fairies but mice,' echoed Santa Claus.

He reached up to the mouse stockings and in each he dropped a diamond. At least, the tiny things sparkled like diamonds but they may have been magic dewdrops.

'It was lots of mice who did it, and a good kind spider and my humble self,' added the cat.

'Then, Mistress Cat, you shall have a present,'

said Santa and he fastened a white velvet collar with a scarlet tassel round the cat's neck and to the spider he gave a tiny crown of rubies.

Then the clock struck twelve, midnight, and Christmas Day came. The mice faded away into their holes, each with his little furry stockings, the spider placed her crown on her head and she returned to her web. The cat lay down by the empty grate, and Santa Claus took up his sack.

He climbed up the chimney and went to the reindeer. 'Christmas Day is here, and even the lowliest creatures have remembered. Come along, my reindeer. Gallop. Gallop to take the good news of Christmas.'

And they flew up in the sky and continued their long journey.

The Fairy Ship

Little Tom was the son of a sailor. He lived in a small whitewashed cottage in Cornwall, on the rocky cliffs looking over the sea. From his bedroom window he could watch the great waves with their curling plumes of white foam, and count the seagulls as they circled in the blue sky. The water went right away to the dim horizon, and sometimes Tom could see the smoke from ships like a dark flag in the distance. Then he ran to get his spy-glass, to get a better view.

Tom's father was somewhere out on that great stretch of ocean, and all Tom's thoughts were there, following him, wishing for him to come home. Every day he ran down the narrow path to the small rocky bay, and sat there waiting for the ship to return. It was no use to tell him that a ship could not enter the tiny cove with its sharp needles of rocks and dangerous crags. Tom was certain that he would see his sailor father step out to the strip of sand if he kept watch. It seemed the proper way to come home.

December brought wild winds that swept the coast. Little Tom was kept indoors, for the gales would have blown him away like a gull's feather if he had gone to the rocky pathway. He was deeply disappointed that he couldn't keep watch in his favourite place. A letter had come, saying that his father was on his way home and any time he might arrive. Tom feared he wouldn't be there to see him, and he stood by the window for hours watching the sky and the wild tossing sea.

'What shall I have for Christmas, Mother?' he asked one day. 'Will Father Christmas remember to bring me something?'

'Perhaps he will, if our ship comes home in time,' smiled his mother, and then she sighed and looked out at the wintry scene.

'Will he come in a sleigh with eight reindeer pulling it?' persisted Tom.

'Maybe he will,' said his mother, but she wasn't thinking what she was saying. Tom knew at once, and he pulled her skirt.

'Mother! I don't think so. I don't think he will,' said he.

'Will what, Tom? What are you talking about?'

'Father Christmas won't come in a sleigh, because there isn't any snow here. Besides, it is too rocky, and the reindeer would slip. I think he'll come in a ship, a grand ship with blue sails and a gold mast.'

Little Tom took a deep breath and his eyes shone.

'Don't you think so, Mother? Blue sails, or maybe red ones. Satin like our parlour cushion.

My father will come back with him. He'll come in a ship full of presents, and Father Christmas will give him some for me.'

Tom's mother suddenly laughed aloud.

'Of course he will, little Tom. Father Christmas comes in a sleigh drawn by a team of reindeer to the children of towns and villages, but to the children of the sea he sails in a ship with all the presents tucked away in the hold.'

She took her little son up in her arms and kissed him, but he struggled away and went back to the window.

'I'm going to be a sailor soon,' he announced proudly. 'Soon I shall be big enough, and then I shall go over the sea.'

He looked out at the stormy sea where his father was sailing, every day coming nearer home, and on that wild water he saw only mist and spray, and the cruel waves dashing over the jagged splinters of rock.

Christmas morning came, and it was a day of surprising sunshine and calm. The seas must have known it was Christmas and they kept peace and goodwill. They danced into the cove in sparkling waves, and fluttered their flags of white foam, and tossed their treasures of seaweed and shells on the narrow beach.

Tom awoke early, and looked in his stocking on the bed-post. There was nothing in it at all! He wasn't surprised. Land children had their presents dropped down the chimney, but he, a sailor's son, had to wait for the ship. The stormy weather had kept the Christmas ship at sea, but now she was bound to come.

His mother's face was happy and excited, as if she had a secret. Her eyes shone with joy, and she seemed to dance round the room in excitement, but she said nothing.

Tom ate his breakfast quietly – a bantam egg and some honey for a special treat. Then he ran outside, to the gate, and down the slippery grassy path which led to the sea.

'Where are you going, Tom?' called his mother. 'You wait here, and you'll see something.'

'No, Mother. I'm going to look for the ship, the little Christmas ship,' he answered, and away he trotted, so his mother turned to the house, and made her own preparations for the man she loved. The tide was out and it was safe now the winds had dropped.

She looked through the window, and she could see the little boy sitting on a rock on the sand, staring away at the sea. His gold hair was blown back, his blue jersey was wrinkled about his stout little body. The gulls swooped round him as he tossed scraps of bread to feed them. Jackdaws came whirling from the cliffs and a raven croaked hoarsely from its perch on a rocky peak.

The water was deep blue, like the sky, and purple shadows hovered over it, as the waves gently rocked the cormorants fishing there. The little boy leaned back in his sheltered spot, and the sound of the water made him drowsy. The sweet air lulled him and his head began to droop.

Then he saw a sight so beautiful he had to rub his eyes to get the sleep out of them. The wintry sun made a pathway on the water, flickering with points of light on the crests of the waves, and down this golden lane came a tiny ship that seemed no larger than a toy. She moved swiftly through the water, making for the cove, and Tom cried out with joy and clapped his hands as she approached.

The wind filled the blue satin sails, and the sunbeams caught the mast of gold. On deck was a company of sailors dressed in white, and they were making music of some kind, for shrill squeaks and whistles and pipings came through the air. Tom leaned forward to watch them, and as the ship came nearer he could see that the little sailors were playing flutes, tootling a hornpipe, then whistling a carol.

He stared very hard at their pointed faces, and little pink ears. They were not sailor-men at all, but a crew of white mice! There were four-and-twenty of them – yes, twenty-four white mice with gold rings round their snowy necks, and gold rings in their ears!

The little ship sailed into the cove, through the barriers of sharp rocks, and the white mice hurried backward and forward, hauling at the silken ropes, casting the gold anchor, crying with high voices as the ship came to port close to the rock where Tom sat waiting and watching.

Out came the Captain – and would you believe it? He was a Duck, with a cocked hat like Nelson's, and a blue jacket trimmed with gold braid. Tom knew at once he was Captain Duck because under his wing he carried a brass telescope, and by his side was a tiny sword.

He stepped boldly down the gangway and waddled to the eager little boy.

'Quack! Quack!' said the Captain, saluting Tom, and Tom of course stood up and saluted back.

'The ship's cargo is ready, Sir,' said the Duck. 'We have sailed across the sea to wish you a merry Christmas. You will find everything in order, Sir. My men will bring the merchandise ashore, and here is the Bill of Lading.'

The Duck held out a piece of seaweed, and Tom took it. 'Thank you, Captain Duck,' said he. 'I'm not a very good reader yet, but I can count up to twenty-four.'

'Quack! Quack!' cried the Duck, saluting again. 'Quick! Quick!' he said, turning to the ship, and the four-and-twenty white mice scurried down to the cabin and dived into the hold.

Then up on deck they came, staggering under their burdens, dragging small bales of provisions, little oaken casks, baskets, sacks and hampers. They raced down the ship's ladders, and clambered over the sides, and swarmed down the gangway. They brought their packages ashore and laid them on the smooth sand near Tom's feet.

There were almonds and raisins, bursting from silken sacks. There were sugar-plums and goodies, pouring out of wicker baskets. There was a host of tiny toys, drums and marbles, tops and balls, pearly shells, and a flying kite, a singing bird and a musical-box.

When the last toy had been safely carried from the ship the white mice scampered back. They weighed anchor, singing 'Yo-heave-ho!' and they ran up the rigging. The Captain cried 'Quack! Quack!' and he stood on the ship's bridge. Before Tom could say 'Thank you', the little golden ship

began to sail away, with flags flying, and the blue satin sails tugging at the silken cords. The four-and-twenty white mice waved their sailor hats to Tom, and the Captain looked at him through his spy-glass.

Away went the ship, swift as the wind, a glittering speck on the waves. Away she went towards the far horizon along that bright path that the sun makes when it shines on water.

Tom waited till he could see her no more, and then he stooped over his presents. He tasted the almonds and raisins, he sucked the goodies, he

beat the drum, and tinkled the musical-box and the iron triangle. He flew the kite, and tossed the balls in the air, and listened to the song of the singing-bird. He was so busy playing that he did not hear soft footsteps behind him.

Suddenly he was lifted up in a pair of strong arms and pressed against a thick blue coat, and two bright eyes were smiling at him.

'Well, Thomas, my son! Here I am! You didn't expect me, now did you? A Happy Christmas, Tom, boy. I crept down soft as a snail, and you never heard a tinkle of me, did you?'

'Oh, Father!' Tom flung his arms round his father's neck and kissed him many times. 'Oh, Father. I knew you were coming. Look! They've been, they came just before you, in the ship.'

'Who, Tom? Who's been? I caught you fast asleep. Come along home and see what Father Christmas has brought you. He came along o' me, in my ship, you know. He gave me some presents for you.'

'He's been here already, just now, in a little gold ship, Father,' cried Tom, stammering with excitement. 'He's just sailed away. He was a Duck, Captain Duck, and there were four-and-twenty white mice with him. He left me all these toys. Lots of toys and things.'

Tom struggled to the ground, and pointed to the sand, but where the treasure of the fairy ship had been stored there was only a heap of pretty shells and seaweed and striped pebbles.

'They's all gone,' he cried, choking back a sob, but his father laughed and carried him off, pick-a-back, up the narrow footpath to the cottage.

'You've been dreaming, my son,' said he. 'Father Christmas came with me, and he's brought you a fine lot of toys, and I've got them at home for you.'

'Didn't dream,' insisted Tom. 'I saw them all.'

On the table in the kitchen lay such a medley of presents that Tom opened his eyes wider than ever. There were almonds and raisins, and goodies in little coloured sacks, and a musical-box with a picture of a ship on its round lid. There was a drum with scarlet edges, and a book, and a pearly shell from a far island, and a kite of thin paper from China, and a love-bird in a cage. Best of all there was a little model of his father's ship, which his father had carved for Tom.

'Why, these are like the toys from the fairy ship,' cried Tom. 'Those were very little ones, like fairy toys, and these are big ones, real ones.'

'Then it must have been a dream-ship,' said his mother. 'You must tell us all about it.'

So little Tom told the tale of the ship with blue satin sails and gold mast, and he told of the four-and-twenty white mice with gold rings round their necks, and the Captain Duck, who said 'Quack! Quack!' His father sat listening, as the words came tumbling from the excited little boy.

When Tom had finished, the sailor said, 'I'll

sing you a song of that fairy-ship, our Tom. Then you'll never forget what you saw.'

He waited a moment, gazing into the great fire on the hearth, and then he stood up and sang this song to his son and to his wife.

> There was a ship a-sailing,
> A-sailing on the sea.
> And it was deeply laden,
> With pretty things for me.
>
> There were raisins in the cabin,
> And almonds in the hold,
> The sails were made of satin,
> And the mast it was of gold.
>
> The four-and-twenty sailors
> That stood between the decks
> Were four-and-twenty white mice
> With rings about their necks.
>
> The Captain was a Duck, a Duck,
> With a jacket on his back,
> And when this fairy-ship set sail,
> The Captain he said 'Quack'.

'Oh, sing it again,' cried Tom, clapping his hands, and his father sang once more the song that later became a nursery rhyme.

It was such a lovely song that Tom hummed it all that happy Christmas Day, and it just fitted into the tune on his musical-box. He sang it to his children when they were little, long years later, and you can sing it too if you like!

The Holly Bears a Berry

It was December, the fields were bare, and the sheep were safe in the folds. The great woods spread their rimed network of branches over the little ice-covered pools. Flocks of chaffinches darted through the crystal air, playing their winter game of hide-and-seek in their favourite trees. A little brook tinkled cheerfully as it ran through ice flakes and ferny snow-flowers.

A young man walked along the narrow tracks in the woodland. In his hand was a bill-hook and on his back a rope. He wore a brown coat the colour of the dead beech leaves and his fustian trousers were tied at the knees. Round his neck was a scarf as blue as his eyes. He was seeking holly, for he had promised his young wife that he would get her a bunch of berries for Christmas.

'You'll not find one berry,' said she laughing at him, as she stood at the door of the cottage by the wood. 'There's ne'er a red berry this year. I've kept my eyes open when I've been out walking, but I've never seen a glimmer of one.

We've got ivy and yew and bay, and we must be content with holly leaves.'

'I'll find a berry for you, Jenny, sure as I'm a woodman. It wouldn't be Christmas with no holly berries to decorate the kitchen. There will surely be some in the forest on the old trees I know far away. I'll give you a surprise, Jenny Wren.'

She laughed again at his words. Jenny Wren was Timothy's name for her, for he said she was as spry as a little bird and she sang as sweetly as any wren in the hedge as she went about her work in the kitchen.

'Good-bye, Jenny Wren,' called Timothy, and away he went into the wood.

Jenny went back to the kitchen to scrub the table white as a bone, and polish the handles of the chest, and prepare for Christmas. The room was as neat as a little bird's nest, with warm curtains and shutters, and little rugs on the floor. There was a good fire burning, and by the side of it was a cradle. Jenny stooped over it, and rocked it for a few minutes, singing very softly.

There lay her baby son, young Timothy. It was his first Christmas, and it was fitting that everything should be beautiful for him.

So Jenny baked a batch of new bread, and filled the mince-pies and sang a carol to her baby, while Timothy went on his quest.

Timothy walked boldly into the woods, making for the grove of holly trees which had been spangled with ripe berries in other years. When he reached the dark green trees he was disappointed. They stood serene, glittering in the wintry sunshine with a point of light on every sharp leaf, but never a berry grew there. Timothy searched them, but he had no reward. He went on, farther into the woods, taking a bearing of his direction now and again, tracking the hollies which grew in friendly companies here and there. He walked for miles, and the feeling of disappointment deepened. He couldn't bear to return empty-handed. It was strange that there were no holly berries in the crowds of trees which lived in the vast woods.

Then he saw a gold-crested bird with green plumage and scarlet wing feathers flying through the trees. It rested on a holly, and as he crept up to it he saw that the tree was covered with fruit which the bird was devouring. He raised his hand to scare it away, and then he stopped. It was so beautiful he had not the heart to disturb it. On Christmas Eve such a bird must surely be a sacred bird, perhaps flown from the East with the Wise Men, a part of the miracle of Christmas. So he watched the bird as it hopped among the glossy leaves and stripped the tree.

The bird watched him also, its bright eyes stared unwinking at him, it turned its head and showed off its brilliant plumage. It flirted its tail feathers and ruffled its wings as if to display all its beauty.

'I'll tell Jenny Wren about it. Never was there such a bird! It must have flown from foreign lands, from India, or China, or the hills of Bethlehem,' said Timothy to himself.

Then he was aware that somebody besides himself was watching the bird. Under the tree stood a man, shadowed by the green boughs. He wore a green pointed hood on his head and green leather jacket and long jack-boots. Over his shoulder was a fleece of white wool or snow, Timothy could not be sure, but it glistened like hoar-frost in the sun. His face was wrinkled and old, creased and puckered in a thousand brown lines. He held a staff in his hand, and Timothy saw that it was made of holly wood. It was spiked with broken branches, and the bark was stripped to show the white wood in a pattern of green and white. His hands were thin and his fingers were sharp as a bird's claws.

He began to sing in a clear voice, sweet as an angel's:

> The holly and the ivy,
> When they are both full grown,
> Of all the trees that are in the wood,
> The holly bears the crown.

Then he gave a shrill piercing whistle and the bird flew down and perched on his arm, with sharp beak pressed against him.

Timothy stared, both at the wondrous beauty of the bird and the strange appearance of the old man.

'You be looking for holly berries?' asked the man.

'Yes, sir,' replied Timothy. 'Your bird seems to have a liking for them, for I've found never an odd berry in all these woods.'

'They are his food. They belong to him, from time immemorial.'

'I've never seen such a bird before,' said Timothy.

'No, and you wouldn't have seen him today if it hadn't been Christmas Eve, and the moon young, and the star in the sky.'

Timothy looked up and in the green-blue sky in the West he saw the thin young crescent moon and one bright star.

'If you want some berries, I will give you some, for you'll not find any by yourself this year. It is only once in a hundred years we come for them.'

Timothy could well believe it, for the man looked so old he might have been one of the ancient trees come to life.

'I'll give you some berries better than any others,' said the man, stepping back to the great holly tree, and the bird balanced on his arm and fluttered its lovely wings.

The old man reached up to the holly tree, and drew down a branch which had three berries growing on it. Timothy hadn't seen them, but they shone like burning fire in the glossy leaves.

'Three holly berries. One for you and one for your wife and one for the babe in the cradle,' said the old man, holding out the branch to Timothy.

'How did you know I have a wife and baby?' asked Timothy astonished.

'I can read men's minds,' said the ancient man, and he stroked the bright feathers of the bird, and laid his withered cheek on the soft wings. 'I know you are Timothy Snow, and your father was Timothy Snow, killed by a falling tree, and your son is Timothy also. I could tell you other things, but that is enough.'

'Who are you?' asked Timothy. 'You're a stranger in these parts surely, for I've lived here for all my twenty years, and never set eyes on you before. Are you shepherd at one of the hill farms away yonder? They have an old man working there.'

'I'm a shepherd from over the hills, from a distant land. I'm a shepherd wandering the earth, returning at Christmas for a brief visit to my flocks of green trees.'

'And what may you be called?' asked Timothy.

'Holly is my name. Old Holly, once young Holly, and that was when King Henry was on the throne. My father was Old Holly, too.'

'And the bird?' asked Timothy, and he stretched out a hand to touch the bird's feathers. Quickly he drew back, for they were sharp as thorns. Then he saw that every feather was like a holly leaf with pointed edge upturned.

'He is a Holly Bird,' said the old man. 'He lives with me in the heart of the unseen world. And now I will bid you good day, and may good fortune favour you this Christmas.'

'A happy Christmas to you, Old Holly, sir,' called Timothy. The old man moved slowly away under the drooping boughs of the great holly trees. The branches dipped to the earth, and as the old man walked under he disappeared as completely as if he had stepped into the hearts of the trees. Timothy lifted the leaves and stepped after him, but the beautiful bird and the old man had gone. There was no sign or shadow, only a green feather lay there, pricked and jagged like a holly leaf.

So Timothy put the holly bough with the three scarlet berries on his shoulder and started off towards home. Only three berries for Jenny Wren, and for little Timothy, but what a tale he had to tell! He would tell it over and over again, with details of the old man's coat and long boots, and fleece like snow and eyes bright as stars in the wrinkled face, and the bird with its barbed feathers and its topaz eyes and its crest of gold. Jenny Wren would open her brown eyes and gaze at him, but she would understand something that was hidden, an unknown mystery. So back he went to the cottage. It was dark when Timothy reached home, but Jenny Wren had lighted the lamp and left the shutters unclosed, so that a gold beam streamed over the field to meet him. His heart was warmed as he trudged towards that beam of joy where little Timothy lay snug in his cradle.

He had been farther into the woods than he realized, he had walked many miles and there was only the holly branch to show. As he walked up the garden path the door was flung open and Jenny Wren rushed out and threw her arms around him.

'Oh, Timothy. I thought you were lost,' she cried, burying her face in his thick coat. 'Where have you been all day, and where's the holly?'

'Jenny my love, this is all I've brought – three holly berries!' said he sadly.

'Three holly berries,' echoed Jenny, taking the glistening bough of dark leaves with their three jewels of berries. 'Only this after a day in the woods!'

'Never mind,' she added quickly when Timothy's face fell. 'There's one for me and one for you and one for baby Timothy.'

'That's what Old Holly said when he gave me the bough,' said Timothy. 'I'll tell you my tale while I have supper. Then we'll hang up our decorations, for I've walked many a mile and I'm tired.'

So Timothy ate his Christmas Eve supper of green sage-cheese and mince-pies and hot posset, which he drank in the two-handled posset mug, and as he ate and drank he told the tale of the woods, of the ancient man, whose name was Holly, and the bright Holly Bird which flitted through the trees. Jenny sat with her arms on the table, listening wide-eyed to her husband.

'Well, it is certainly a lovely bit of holly! Even if there are only three berries to decorate our room, they are the best I've ever seen, and the leaves glitter like polished brass,' said Jenny, when her husband had finished. 'He must have been one of those folk of other days you hear of sometimes, come back to earth. Well, I've got some streamers of ivy and some yew and bay. We will make a kissing-bunch and put those berries in it. Then everyone who comes will see them.'

• So they decorated the kitchen, and strung the sprays of ivy round the coloured almanacks on the wall, and put yew over the grandfather clock in the corner, and branches of smooth sweet-smelling bay among the shining saucepans on the shelf. The holly they twisted in a round bunch, with a couple of flags and a glass bell and apples and oranges on it, and that was the kissing-bunch. They hung it from the hook in the middle of the low ceiling, and then they kissed one another beneath it.

Whether it was the candlelight, or the flickering fire, or the ardour of their kisses I do not know, but those three holly berries shone like scarlet flames. They glowed with a light of their own which put the candles to shame, and the little room seemed to be full of dancing shadows and flickering points of flame, coming from the three lovely holly berries in the kissing-bunch.

Even when Timothy blew out the candles to save the candle-wax and sat in the dusky light, the berries shone and every leaf of holly sent out a gleam like a star. There was a sweet fragrance in the air, and a soft ringing of bells, but when Jenny asked Timothy if he noticed these things he said the sweetness was from Jenny Wren's brown hair, and the ringing of the bells was in their hearts.

'Nay! I'm sure there is a faraway bell ringing,' said Jenny, as she sat in the firelight and held Timothy's hand.

She watched the shadows moving on the wall, and as she looked she saw an age-old story, for out of the darkness came three men, hooded figures, who moved across the room and hovered near the cradle, bending low to it, holding out their long, thin hands with gifts.

'Look! Look! The Three Wise Men,' she whispered awestruck, but Timothy's eyes were shut, he was fast asleep after the long walk. Only the mother saw the vision of the East.

The three shadows knelt there, and others came crowding round, men with shepherds' crooks in their hands. Soft bells rang more clearly and the sweetness in the little room was like incense. Then the shadows arose and went their way, moving across the whitewashed wall and fading in the firelight.

Christmas Day was the happiest Timothy could remember, and Jenny Wren agreed with him that never had she felt such bliss as filled her heart.

They were too far from a church to go there with the baby, but they sang their Christmas hymn together and said their Christmas prayer. Timothy gave Jenny a little silver locket which he had bought in the town when he went to sell his wood, and Jenny gave Timothy the thick white stockings and scarf which she had knitted for him and embroidered with scarlet holly berries and leaves. Then little Timothy received his presents, a lamb carved from a piece of white holly wood, which Big Timothy had made secretly, whittling it with his knife when he had his dinner among the trees. Jenny gave her little son a pair of tiny white slippers, woven from sheep's wool, tied with red ribbons.

The baby crowed and laughed over his presents, but he stretched up his hand to the kissing-bunch. He leapt in Timothy's arms when he was held up to see the silvery bell and shining ball of glass.

'It's the berries he's after. Look, Timothy. Look how bright they are!' cried Jenny.

The holly berries glowed like three fires in the kissing-bunch. They seemed larger and finer even than the night before, and they flamed as if a hidden beacon were there. Both Timothy and Jenny stared at them in silence, and little Timothy leapt and crowed and chuckled with tiny fat hands upraised to them.

'Let him have them,' said Timothy. 'See, I'll pick them off, and hold them in my hand for him to look at.'

He gathered the three berries and held them in the palm of his hand. Jenny stooped over them, breathing the exquisite smell which came from them. The baby was forgotten, for the berries were expanding as they slowly opened.

The scarlet skins cracked asunder, and the sweet fragrance filled the room. It curled up like blue smoke, and hung in the shape of a holly tree with pointed leaves and a crown of thorns on the top. The berries dropped apart, with skin back-turned to show their hidden treasures. In one lay a bag of gold dust. In another a casket of frankincense. In the third a pot of sweet myrrh.

'Gold, Frankincense and Myrrh,' murmured Jenny. 'In memory of the first Christmas Day, Timothy.'

Jenny put the miracles away in the oak chest, each wrapped in the scarlet skin of its berry. They were gifts for their little child. The past was to be a present to bring hope for the future.

Every Christmas Timothy told the tale of the strange happenings in the deep wood, and Jenny showed the beautiful gifts to little Timothy. Some times father and son walked through the woods seeking the trees where Old Holly had waited with the flaming bird on his arm, but they never saw him again.

Tom Tit and the Fir-Tree

Little Tom Tit and tall Fir-tree
Sang a carol joyously.
Tom Tit whistled with elfin might,
The stars peeped down to see the sight.
Fir-tree waved his plumes serene,
Plucked his harp with fingers green,
Sang to the Holy Ones above,
A Christmas carol of Peace and Love.
Frost and glitter on meadow and lea,
Little Tom Tit and tall Fir-tree.

'There!' cried the Tom Tit, as he stopped to take breath. 'That's as grand a music as ever came out of this wood. The oaks and the great beeches couldn't do better. I should think the sound of it has gone twice round the world. What do you think, Fir-tree? Wasn't it a splendid music that we made?'

The tall Fir-tree nodded his shaggy head, and sighed in the wind, and the murmur of his sighing was like the roaring of the sea.

'The stars are out, Tom Tit,' he boomed in his deep voice. 'Orion the Hunter is climbing the sky with his belt all a-glitter. The Dog Stars are racing around, and there's the Hare crouching before them. The Great Bear is prowling in the fields of heaven, and Aldebaran is winking his red eye. It's dangerous for a little bird like you to be abroad. You'd best be off to bed, Tom Tit.'

The little blue Tit swung lightly on the bough, and peeked up impudently at the Great Bear marching in the night sky. That furry golden Bear would never catch *him*, for it moved so slowly only the solemn old Fir-tree could see its motion, and of course the tree watched all through the winter, whereas the Tom Tit could fly away like blue lightning.

'Be off to bed, young Tom Tit. It is Christmas Eve, and mysteries are abroad,' bellowed the Fir-tree, as the wind caught it and tossed its boughs. 'Birds and beasts should be a-bed, and the trees will watch the sky alone tonight.'

Tom Tit crept into an ivy bush, and put his head under his wing in the warm shelter of the large thick leaves. Then he fell asleep, but every now and then he awoke, and opened one bright eye to peer about like a child who wants to catch Santa Claus, for the Tom Tit wished to get a glimpse of the happenings that the Fir-tree had told him about. It was the Holy Night, the Fir-tree said, and a star travelled across the sky bringing tidings of joy, and all the heavens sang, just as Fir-tree and Tom Tit had carolled together.

So the Tom Tit put his head from under his wing and kept his beady eye on the dark-blue sky, watching.

The earth appeared to be sleeping, but in reality it was more watchful than in the daytime. Every blade of grass in the wide pastures, every leafless tree in the wood, moved softly, stretching upward and then bowing down.

The Fir-tree stood very straight and majestical, with its dark branches vibrant, as it looked at the wonders, and the little Tom Tit gazed entranced.

He saw the moon sail along the sky like a splendid ship and on deck there was a host of shining angels with trumpets and horns, singing and playing the heavenly music, cold and clear and far away. The ship moved through the blue air, journeying to some unknown port.

Meteorites shot down, leaving long trails of gold, until they disappeared among the darkly watching trees of the woods on the horizon. The Tom Tit saw the twinkling changing colours of the great stars, but the Fir-tree hailed them as friends. They were the familiar winter stars, great Aldebaran, and blue Rigel, the Bull with his round eye, and the prancing Goat, Capella. The Fir-tree knew them all like his own sisters and brothers in the fir wood, for ever since he was a seedling tree he had whispered to them in the night, watching for them to appear above the skyline.

Across the dome above him swept the broad

band of the Milky Way, a white pathway of stars, and the Fir-tree could see the millions of worlds like silver sand which made it. Down that pale road came a company of angels, flying towards the earth, singing as they came, and the sound of their voices, thin and sweet, was mingled with the nearer music of the host on the slowly sailing ship of the moon.

The Fir-tree turned away from these and searched the skies for something else. He stared towards the east, longingly, and the little Tom Tit leaned from his ivy shelter to look too. Suddenly the Fir-tree saw what he had waited for ever since he and the little bird had sung their carol. Out of the blue depths came a star with five points, brilliant, moving rapidly. It was the Star of Bethlehem which appears each Christmas Eve in memory of the First Christmas.

It travelled across the jewelled sky and came to rest over the great square tower of the old church in the village. There it hung like a lantern to guide wanderers home, and every stone in the tower shone under its light. After it came the moonship with its angel passengers, and the moon dropped its anchor in the churchyard. Then all the little angels came fluttering out, and some of them perched on the tower, and stayed there, round-faced and rosy-winged cherubs. Others entered the church, for every window and door was wide open, and a radiance came from within.

Although the Fir-tree never moved, for his

roots went deep among the rocks of the earth, yet he could see the scene inside the holy place as clearly as if he were there. But the little Tom Tit sprang from his shelter and flew like a blue arrow to the doorway, where he hid behind the carving and watched.

The cherubs rustled their rosy wings and floated up the aisle to the altar, and all the tall angels from the Milky Way followed after them, with never a sound, except the music of their voices. There lay a little Babe in a cradle of straw, and His wide-open eyes looked up at His visitors, who floated around like the snow-flakes of a celestial snow-storm, pure and cold and beautiful.

Through the open door streamed more and more angels, as the Milky Way gave up its myriads of travellers. The music grew louder and the angels adored the Little One lying there, while from the woods came a rustling and murmuring as the trees joined in the praise.

Then an astonishing thing happened. There was a flutter of earthly wings and a beating of the air, and through the church came a flock of birds. They perched on the altar, and filled the choir stalls, where on Sundays rosy-faced boys from the cottages sat demure with white surplices covering their best Sunday clothes. The birds looked like choirboys, with their round heads and bright eager eyes and chattering tongues. There were thrushes and blackbirds, chaffinches and sparrows, robins and starlings – just the common little birds of the countryside, and they were led by the blue Tom Tit, who had fetched his friends and neighbours to join the angels.

The Fir-tree shook his branches with amazement at the boldness and impudence of the birds, who had gone where no living creature dared to move in that heavenly host, but the Babe held out His little hands and called to them.

Then the birds sang their own carol of Christmas, so shrill and piping, with multitudinous whistlings and chirpings and twitterings, the noise of it drowned even the sweet song of the angels. But the Babe laughed and stroked the feathers of the blue Tom Tit, who was their leader, and the Tit swung from the altar rails and turned a somersault for the Child.

All this the Fir-tree saw as he stood in the starlit wood one Christmas Eve, and watched the Star of Bethlehem hanging over the old village church, and to me he told the story.

The Kissing-Bunch

It was Christmas Eve. On the kitchen floor stood the large clothes-basket, but instead of sheets and towels it was heaped with holly and ivy which had been cut in the woods that same afternoon. The farmer and his man had been out with knives and a short axe to gather the Christmas harvest. The green leaves glittered, the berries shone like little red fires. There was a strong rich smell of the wild woods which seemed to have entered the house with the branches of the trees.

The bare scrubbed table had been cleared, and at one end of it Mrs Dale made the mince-pies. That was part of Christmas Eve, and everyone had a share in the making. So many things were happening at once, the children scarcely knew where to turn.

Elizabeth and her brother Thomas danced and shouted with joy, they ran round the long table, and crept under it, between the Windsor chairs, and they sat hidden on the stone floor, as they played.

'Come along, children. You have the

decorating to do. You asked to be allowed to do it,' their mother reminded them.

They came out and stood watching her for a few minutes, eager to taste the mincemeat. Mrs Dale rolled the pastry with swift smooth strokes of the great wooden rolling-pin that had been used for a hundred years. Then she took the patty-pans from the heap on the table. The children had already sorted them for her. There were big patty-pans for farm workers, and tiny ones for children, and fluted ones for visitors and nice ordinary ones for everyday for everybody.

'You can put the mincemeat in, Tabitha Ann,' she called to her youngest child, and little Tabitha Ann shook back her yellow curls, and came slowly from the corner of the oak settle where she had been staring at the holly and the ivy. She was a dreamy girl, unlike her sister Elizabeth and her brother Thomas. She was wondering what the holly thought when it found itself not growing in the deep dark wood, but here in the bright hot kitchen of the farm. She was listening for the leaves to tinkle and speak.

She climbed on the high stool by the table and measured the fragrant spicy mincemeat from the great brown crock into the pastry-lined patty-pans, and as she dipped her spoon she whispered to herself.

'One for you,' said she, to a patty-pan. 'One

for you, and one for you. One for the holly, and one for the ivy, and one for the mistletoe man. One for an angel, and one for a fairy, and one for Tabitha Ann.'

Then she looked up at her mother with shining eyes. 'Mother, I've made a poem,' said she.

'Have you, my dear?' Mrs Dale was too busy to bother over poems and Tabitha Ann murmured her words under her breath.

> One for the holly, and one for the
>   ivy,
> And one for the mistletoe man.
> One for an angel, and one for a fairy,
> And one for Tabitha Ann.

Elizabeth and Thomas began to decorate the room. They cut off small twigs of holly berries and placed them behind each shining silvery dish-cover which hung in a row on the kitchen wall. There was a grandfather dish-cover large enough to cover a couple of turkeys at one end, and a baby dish-cover for a couple of poached eggs at the other end, and in between were all the old dish-covers of graduated size. Each carried its own spray of red berries to glitter in its metal mirror.

Then the children put holly and berries between the flower-painted plates of the dresser, and every plate on the plate-rack, every lustre jug hanging from the shelves had its own small decoration of holly. They climbed on the tall stools to reach and little Tabitha Ann watched them, while she ladled the spoonfuls of mincemeat and sang very softly her poem.

When they had finished that side of the room the oak dresser was like a screen from the greenwood, with berries and leaves and pretty plates and jugs.

Next they mounted to the mantelpiece, over the wide fireplace, and Thomas held the stool while Elizabeth balanced herself on the hearth. High up among the brass candlesticks, the copper pans and dishes and the two china dogs, they put their ivy sprays and ivy berries.

Tabitha Ann paused in her work to see that no object was forgotten. Christmas Eve belongs to everything, to pots and pans, to furniture and pictures. It is eternal, and the woods and the fields share the festival.

'Does it look nice, Mother?' called Elizabeth, turning round from her high perch. The hearth-stone was worn and uneven, and the stool was unsteady, so that Thomas had to hold it very firmly as it rocked on the old stones.

'Beautiful, my dear; but you want a piece of holly in the copper kettle spout,' laughed Mrs Dale, pointing to her little ancient tea-kettle up there.

All round the kitchen the two children went, putting their holly sprays on every pan and copper saucepan and measure and pot. Even the flitches of bacon that hung on one of the walls, curing for the winter's supply, had their pieces of holly, to glisten in the white saltpetre that lay on their sides.

Along the top of the grandfather clock they wove sprays of ivy, and over the tall oak cupboard with its carved doors they fastened their best pieces, taking care the doors would open. It would never do if the holly fell down each time the cups and saucers were taken from the cupboard shelves.

'It's like a fairy-tale house,' said Elizabeth, and little Tabitha Ann echoed, 'Fairy-tale house. Yes. They'll come here now, little angels and fairies.'

Elizabeth took no notice; she went on with her decoration, and Thomas cut the holly and handed it to her. The little looking-glass where the farm man brushed his hair, and the painted tin case where his brush was kept, each must have a scrap of holly in honour of Christmas Day.

'Tabitha Ann, make a cross in each mince-pie,' said Mrs Dale, who had now covered each little pie with a neat pastry cover, edged with curling fringe. She glanced at her solemn little daughter, whose eyes wandered from table to walls as she tried to see everything at once.

Tabitha cut a tiny cross for God Himself in the pastry lids. Then Mrs Dale opened wide the great deep oven in the side of the fireplace and carried the trays of pies to be cooked.

'What next?' asked Elizabeth. 'Can we have the lanterns now, Mother?'

'Yes, the lanterns! The lanterns!' cried Tabitha Ann. Everything they did was magical to her that night of nights.

'Chinese lanterns,' shouted Thomas, and he lighted a candle ready. They all trooped into the parlour, the dark, mysterious, beautiful room, which was already decorated with holly and ivy. Mrs Dale had done this in the afternoon, and the children held their breath as they looked round. Their mother took her bunch of keys and selected the large shining key with the queer wards. Thomas held the candle while she unlocked her private drawer in the oak chest where she kept her treasures. It was a famous hiding-place, where many beautiful things were kept.

'Let me look too. Let me,' called Tabitha Ann, and she squeezed under her mother's arm, between Thomas and Elizabeth, and peered into the deep drawer. There was a glimpse of leather boxes with gold flowers embossed on them, of Christmas cards with cut paper edges, of a Sunday doll, and a circus panorama, a scrapbook and a silver windmill. From among this collection of bygone toys Mrs Dale took the Chinese paper lanterns, folded like concertinas, painted with gay flowers and scenes, with waterfalls and peonies and Chinese men. There was also a box of coloured candles and a few glass-sided little lanterns from an old Christmas tree.

The children carried them with whoops of excitement, they removed the old candle ends, left from the year before, and fitted the new candles in the sockets. They lighted them and hung them on a cord which stretched across the kitchen ceiling, from two iron hooks. They dangled in a row, delicate, fairy-like lanterns, swinging in the draughts, fluttering with every breath that came whistling through the keyholes of the big old doors. They sent out such a fantastic light, such a shimmer of flowers and soft colours that the children clapped their hands and cried:

'It's really Christmas Eve now.'

There was a good smell of hot mince-pies from the oven, and the rich scent of the holly and the ivy, and a new strange odour from the little twisted candles burning in the magical paper lanterns from China. The bunch of mistletoe swung near, and the candlelight shone on the waxen berries, under the low ceiling. The farm lad, Adam, came in with his pails of new milk frothing to the brim, and Mr Dale followed.

'Look. Look,' cried the children. 'Isn't it beautiful? Christmas Eve and the lanterns lighted.'

They all sat by the fire that night and ate their hot mince-pies and drank their milk. They sang carols, and Adam played a tune on his tin whistle, and Thomas played his little fiddle with many a squeak, and Mr Dale played his concertina.

'Don't forget to hang up your stockings,' called the farmer as the children at last prepared to go to bed. Elizabeth and Thomas laughed, as if they knew a secret, but little Tabitha Ann was very serious.

'Everybody's stocking up,' said she. 'Santa Claus wants everybody's socks and stockings.'

They stamped upstairs carrying their wavering candles and soon there was the sound of shutting doors and little thuds and cries of excitement from the bedrooms above. Mrs Dale ran upstairs to bid each child 'Good night and God bless you'.

That blessing kept them safe from ghosties and goblins and queer things of the night, and Tabitha Ann shut her eyes and slept.

Now in every farmhouse in that part of England a Kissing-bunch was made secretly on Christmas Eve to surprise the children on Christmas morning. For hundreds of years this custom had been kept.

Mr and Mrs Dale planned to make their bunch when the children were fast asleep. So they brought out the best pieces of berried holly, which had been kept apart in the barn, away up the outside steps across the yard. Adam brought the slips of holly indoors, with his lantern swinging, and Mr Dale tied them together in a compact round bunch, arranging them in a double circle of wooden hoops for a frame. The ball was shaped slowly and carefully, with bits tied to the foundation till a beautiful sphere about eighteen inches across was made. It hung from a large hook in the kitchen ceiling.

Mrs Dale had been busy with her ribbons and toys, and now she threaded the scarlet and yellow ribbons among the leaves, so that they dropped in streamers. She tied the silver balls, the red and blue glass bells, by strings which were hidden in the greenery. Little bright flags were stuck in the Kissing-bunch here and there, to remind everyone that Christmas was all over the world. Oranges and the brightest red glossy apples from the orchard store, tangerines and gilded walnuts were slung from threads to hang in the bunch as if they grew there.

It was a magical bush of flowers and fruit, of gold and silver. The oranges and apples caught the light of the lanterns and the blazing fire, the holly leaves glittered and the silver and gold bells and balls were like toys from Paradise.

'Give me the first kiss, my dear,' said Farmer Dale, and he took his wife in his arms and gave her a smacking kiss under the brilliant Kissing-bunch.

'Do you like it, John?' asked Mrs Dale. 'Is it a good one?'

'It's the best you've ever made, my dear,' said Farmer Dale. 'It's as good as the one my own mother made when I was a tiddley little one, and she hung it from the same hook in the ceiling. When she died we had no more Kissing-bunches till I married and the children came.'

'Why didn't you?' asked Mrs Dale, opening wide her brown eyes and clutching her husband's arm.

'We were always too busy. We decorated, of course, but nobody could make a Kissing-bunch.'

They cleared away the scraps of holly from the floor, and tidied up the house for the night. Adam had already gone to his room. They lighted the candle and went to bed, with a backward glance at the beautiful bunch hanging from the ceiling, shining quietly in the light of the dying fire.

Downstairs there was a rustle and a shiver of excitement when the room was empty. The unseen world came to life on Christmas Eve, while the family slept soundly in bed. The grandfather clock ticked more loudly. It cleared its throat with a rumble of wheels; it struck midnight.

The shutters rattled as if someone were shaking them with eager hands. The chairs creaked, and the big armchair tried to speak. Then a little mouse ran over the sanded hearthstone, and the canary awoke in its cage. It flew down from its perch so quickly the cloth fell off and the cage was left uncovered. It began to sing its most melodious song when it spied the Kissing-bunch hanging near it on the next iron hook.

On Christmas Eve! On Christmas Eve!
All the birds and angels sing,
Golden bells and fruits will ring,
On Christmas Eve.

'What's this?' asked the grandfather clock. 'I'm wearing a wreath of holly and ivy. I'm king of the kitchen tonight.'

Then everything seemed to speak at once, and shrill voices came from every direction, from the walls, from the floors, from drawers and dresser and cupboard, as all the world talked.

'We are princesses,' cried the bright dish-covers. 'We are princesses. We wear holly berries in our hair and holly leaves in our hands.'

'We are ballet dancers,' cried the knives and forks and spoons, and they danced out of the tall oak cupboard and fell on the floor. Then they took partners and waltzed round the stones, first on one large flagstone, then on another, stepping daintily over the rag mats so that they did not stumble.

The Chinese lanterns swayed and swung as if the wind blew them. The candles had been extinguished, so they could swing as far as they liked without catching fire. And they sang:

> On Christmas Eve! On Christmas Eve!
> All the lanterns from China sing,
> All the berries and holly leaves ring,
> On Christmas Eve.

The mice picked up a few holly berries, stitched them with tiny stitches, and put them like crowns on their heads.

The chairs rocked slowly backward and forward, as if someone were sitting on them. Indeed the whole room looked as if company were expected. A spider with a diamond crown on its head came out of the corner and began to weave a beautiful web over the bare kitchen table, like a cloth of silver.

The little mice ran swiftly into the cupboard and brought out a few of the smallest mince-pies. The plates slid down from the dresser and set themselves as if for a feast. The jugs with queer faces on their handles, and the lustre jugs with flowers on their golden sides, came quietly down from the dresser hooks and sat on the table. Their grotesque goblin faces smiled and their thick lips opened and shut, and strange gurgling voices came from them, as they murmured unceasingly, 'Christmas Eve! Christmas Eve!'

The flat-irons came lumbering from the corner cupboard, skating on their smooth surfaces over the floor to the hearthstone, where they stopped in amazement and stared up at the Kissing-bunch.

The nutmeg-grater and the egg-beater, the fish-slice and the wooden spoons came clattering down, twirling on their little feet, in a flurry of shining metal and polished wood.

All the time the kitchen familiars were getting ready, preparing for something – all the time the mice were waltzing with their holly berry wreaths on their brows, and the spider was making her silver table-cloth – all the time there was a song and a whistle and a carol and a tune, but louder than everything came the thuds and bangs on the house shutters, as somebody strove to enter.

Suddenly the catch was moved and the wooden shutters were flung back. The window opened a crack, as a tiny white hand entered, and into the room came a blast of wind, a flurry of snow, a shower of hail and a company of lovely little angels.

They flew into the homely old kitchen with feathery wings half closed. Their small thin feet touched the windowsill, they fluttered to the stone sink, and then they reached the floor. Twenty of them appeared, wide-eyed, astonished, with golden tight curls on their heads, with small hands carrying snowballs and snowbells and snow-flowers. Some of them held trumpets and flutes of snow, others had garlands of snow-crystal and frosty blossoms. Some had cakes and fruits of ice, others held rainbow streamers that changed colour as they floated behind the wings of the angels.

They ran round the farm kitchen on tiptoes, with their wings folded behind them, but when a feather touched a jug or a plate there was a shiver of delight in each object that felt the cold, exquisite caress of those heavenly beings.

The grandfather clock ticked very solemnly, trying to keep time, but he had to stop. His hands were still, his brass face stared surprised and bewildered, for Time had gone away and he was in a timeless world of mystery and enchantment.

The happy little angels explored every nook

and hole in the room. They laughed up at the row of dish-covers, each with its twig of holly, and they laughed down at the chairs standing round the big table. They smiled at the spider spinning her silver web to make a cloth, and they smiled at the little mice with their crowns of holly berries.

Then they made a circle holding hands, with wings touching, under the Kissing-bunch, and there they flew round and round, and they blessed the house and all within.

'God bless the house and all who live within,' they sang. 'All the pots and pans, the iron and brass, the holly and the ivy, and the people upstairs. God bless the mouse, the spider, the spoons and forks. God bless all, this night.'

The Kissing-bunch was a flame of lights and colour, and every berry glowed as if a lamp were hidden in its red heart. Every leaf was green as grass in sunshine. The mistletoe berries were like white candles burning high, and the apples and oranges forgot they were only fruit and became apples and oranges from the Garden of Eden.

The angels flew up in the air and hovered around the Kissing-bunch, touching the silver balls and bells, smelling the fruits, listening to the tinkle of the glass bells and the song of the yellow canary in its cage near.

'We must leave a gift for the earth children,' said one angel. 'What shall it be, Brother?'

'I will give kindness of heart,' said an angel,

and into the air it tossed a scented ball that filled the room with perfume.

'I will give love,' said another, and it threw a handful of sparkling rain which fell over all things, covering them with the dew of love.

'I will give riches,' said a third, and it threw a shower of tiny golden coins like sparks into the air.

'I will give poverty,' said a fourth. 'I will give poverty to balance riches, so that the children remember the earth from which they spring.' It tossed a net of pearly light which covered the golden coins and softened their glitter.

'I will give something to the youngest child,' said the smallest angel, who had been peering at the little boots and shoes on the hearth. She stooped down and put a tiny doll with a wooden head and stiff little body into a shoe. It had a wreath of roses on its hair and a pair of gauzy wings.

'What is your gift, Sister?' asked an angel, staring at the toy.

'It's a fairy doll for the child to play with,' said the small angel.

'Would it not be better to give her the gift of Goodness or Wisdom?' asked the angel.

'No. She will find these things in life, but the doll is to make her laugh and to please her,' said the little angel.

Then they pushed wide the window and flew

away, singing their carol of Christmas, so that the children in bed upstairs heard them and murmured in their sleep.

The shutters closed, and the grandfather clock began to tick, and Time moved on. The canary went back to its perch, tucked its head under its wing and fell asleep.

The spoons and forks and knives climbed to their places in the cupboard, and the chairs settled themselves round the table. The jugs went to their hooks on the dresser and closed their little round mouths and shut their eyes. The flat-irons climbed back to the ironing shelf and composed themselves to a long sleep. The nutmeg-grater and the egg-beater and all the kitchen utensils moved away and lay sedately on the bench. The little mice ate up their crowns and hurried away to their holes. The great spider stopped for a moment on the table's edge and regarded the cloth. Over the table-top lay a silver web, a network of lace. She ran down the table, hurried into her crack and rested after her work.

The clock struck six, the cock crew, and the church bells began to ring for the first service in the village church.

Little Tabitha Ann awoke and rubbed her eyes. She got out of bed and felt for her stocking. It was there, filled with odd corners of toys, and Santa Claus had not forgotten her. She struck a match and lighted her candle.

Then, holding the stocking under her arm, she pattered downstairs.

'Merry Christmas. Merry Christmas,' said she to the world.

Nobody answered, and she put down the candle and lifted the latch of the kitchen door. She dropped her Christmas stocking in the effort, but as the door opened she gave a sigh of satisfaction. Christmas had come to the house.

The kitchen was lighted by a dim golden glow that came from the Kissing-bunch where the angels had touched it. Little lights flashed from silver balls and bells, from holly berries and pointed leaves, for each one reflected the candlelight, as she held her candle up to see the sight.

She stood there, under the Kissing-bunch, staring at the lovely things, the flags, the toys, the apples and oranges and gilded nuts.

There was a sweet perfume in the room, and she drank it in, with her small flower-face uplifted. There was a sparkling dew over everything, and she felt a warmth in her heart from it. There was a shimmer of gold and silver caught in a net of mist, but riches and poverty meant nothing to her. She leaned on the table and touched the silver cloth, but it shrank like a cobweb even as her fingers lay upon it. She tasted the frosted flowers and fruits left by the angels, and they dissolved to sweet snow on her lips.

Then she looked at the row of boots and shoes lying on the hearthstone. Something was shining in her own little slipper and she drew out the fairy doll.

'Thank you, angels,' said she.

She picked up her Christmas stocking and the candle and climbed the wooden stairs back to bed. The little fairy doll was clutched tightly in her hand.

'Merry Christmas. Merry Christmas, everybody,' she whispered, and she fell asleep again.

Christmas at Brock the Badger's House

On Christmas Eve Sam Pig was busy decorating the kitchen with holly. All afternoon the little pigs had been out in the woods picking bunches of holly for the great festival. They carried a heap of shining leaves and red berries home, and then they began to make the house as green as the holly bushes. Brock the Badger was away, they had not seen him for a week. He had sent a message that he would return for Christmas, and they felt sure he would come that very night. So they prepared for Christmas Day by themselves.

'Give me that big piece, Ann,' called Sam, as he balanced on top of the steps.

It was a fine piece of holly, and Sam had cut it from the high bough of a tree in the wood. With his own axe he had chopped it and he was proud of it. It was going into the chief place, on top of the shelf where Brock kept his cures and magics and spells.

Sam stretched up, but he couldn't quite reach. He tried again, and then Bill called out, 'Stand on your head, Sam.'

Sam tilted forward and fell headlong on top of his brothers and sister who were waiting below.

'Oh! Oh! Oh!' they shrieked, and there was a whirlwind of scuffling feet and wriggling tails as the four little pigs rolled over in the prickly holly on the floor.

They picked themselves up and sorted themselves out, and rubbed their bruised bodies and took the prickles from their skin.

'I couldn't help it,' cried Sam, indignantly, when Bill was angry with him. 'I didn't fall on purpose.'

'No, you fell on me,' grumbled Bill. 'Let me put it up.'

So away up the steps tripped Bill, but as he leaned over the same thing happened, and down he fell. Luckily the others had kept away and only Bill was hurt.

Then little Ann ran up the ladder, and she was so light and so nimble, she stood on tiptoes and put the holly branch on the shelf in safety.

'Oh, Sam! Sam!' she called, peering in the darkness of the magical shelf. 'I can see something up here.'

'What is it?' asked Sam.

'I don't know. Two eyes are looking at me,' said Ann.

'Nonsense, Ann. There can't be two eyes. Brock doesn't keep eyes up there. I know there's a pot of paint of all colours and a bottle of green ointment and some magical oil and a whistle that calls the wind, but there aren't any eyes.'

Ann came scurrying down. 'Yes. Two eyes, or three or four. Lots of eyes were peeping at me from behind the holly.'

'Nonsense,' said they again, rather nervously, but nobody went up the ladder. Instead they peered from the floor. They thought they saw something blink and wink, but they were not sure. They threw up a pebble and the eyes disappeared, but in a moment they were shining again from the darkness.

Sam ran to the door and looked out across the garden. The snowman was still there, shining in the pale moonlight.

'It isn't the snowman come in,' said he.

'Silly. How could he come in? He'd melt!' cried Bill.

'Never mind,' said Ann. 'Let's get on with the decorating, or Brock will come back and we shan't be ready.'

They hung up the mistletoe, and the Kissing-bunch, with its nuts and apples and a few oranges Mrs Greensleeves, the farmer's wife, had given to Sam. They hung up a picture Sam had painted.

'A MARY XMAS, BROCK!'

it said, in queer crooked letters. Sam read it to his brothers and sister, and as they couldn't read themselves they were quite happy.

They were sitting by the fire cracking nuts and popping corn when there was a thud at the door and Brock came in. He carried a sack on his back and his hat was white with snow.

'Well, little Pigs,' said he, cheerfully. 'You have made a festive room. I'm glad to get back to it. Guess where I've been!'

'To the Big House,' guessed Ann.

'To the market, Brock,' said Sam. 'Did you dare?'

'Yes, I went to the market, and walked about in the crowd and bought lots of things for our Christmas feast. I met Father Christmas, too, and he told me to say that you must not forget to hang up your stockings tonight. When I said you didn't wear stockings, he said your hats would do.'

The little Pigs ran excitedly to get the supper while Brock told his adventures. The market was bright with lamps, and flares, he said. Men were shouting and pushing and nobody saw a dark Badger walking there, with his hat pulled down over his face and scarf over his nose and gloves on his furry paws. Nobody had noticed him, but a policeman had looked very hard. Luckily it was the policeman they all knew, and so he only winked and muttered: 'Goodnight. Happy Christmas, Brock.'

'I popped a Queen Elizabeth shilling in his hand for a present,' added Brock.

Then Brock spoke of the stalls with sweets and toys and turkeys and ducks.

'Wouldn't the fox like to go there!' cried Sam.

'Yes, but he daren't. He hasn't my disguise,' said Brock.

'I like a disguise,' said Sam. 'I should like to go in disguise somewhere, like the Guisers.'

They were eating their supper when there was a shuffle of feet in the snow outside and voices were heard. There was a knock. The little Pigs looked alarmed, but Brock only smiled.

'Open the door, Sam,' said he.

Sam opened a crack and looked out nervously. He saw three figures, cloaked and muffled.

'Please, Sam Pig, we are the Guisers,' said a young voice.

'We've come to sing and act our play for you this Christmas Eve,' said a second voice in a shrill little squeak.

'Guisers,' echoed Sam, enchanted at the thought.

'Guisers,' cried Ann. 'Oh, I've always wanted to see them.'

'Come in,' called Brock, from his corner by the fire. 'Come in, Bold Guisers, and make merry.'

Indoors stepped three little animals, but nobody could see who they were. They had cloaks wrapped round them, and their faces were hidden by black masks with holes through which bright eyes peeped.

Sam glanced up to the high shelf and he could see two green eyes peering down.

'Brock! Brock!' he whispered, but Brock took no notice. The Badger was leaning forward offering the Guisers each a mug of heather ale. They drank without moving their masks, and still no one knew who they were.

'First we'll sing a carol,' said Number One.

They sang 'The Carol of the Cherry Tree', and Sam and the others sang with them.

When they finished there was great applause, but still they kept their faces hidden.

'Now we shall give a play,' said Number One.

'It is called "The Fox and the Hen-roost",' said Number Two.

'That's an ancient play which animals have acted for a thousand years,' said Brock.

'I am the Red Hen,' squeaked a tiny voice.

'I am the Fox,' roared a deep voice.

'I am the Hen-roost and the Tree,' said the third animal. Then they acted the little play:

FOX: 'Come down, come down, my little Red Hen.
Come down from yonder Tree.'

HEN: 'Oh, no! Oh, no!' said the little Red Hen.
'That would be the death of me.'

FOX: 'Come down, come down, my little Red Hen.
Come down and sup with me.'

HEN: 'Oh, no! Oh, no!' said the little Red Hen.
'Your supper I should be.'

FOX: 'Come down, come down, my little Red
Hen.
Come down and marry me.'

HEN: 'Oh, no! Oh, no!' said the little Red Hen.
'Your bride I will never be.'

FOX: 'Come down, come down, my little Red
Hen.
I die for love of thee.'

HEN: 'Then down I'll come,' said the little Red
Hen.
And the Fox, he gobbled she.

The three little animals threw off their masks, and the four little pigs saw Jack Otter, Jim Otter and little Polly Otter, who lived up the river, and once had played with Sam.

They had a merry time, eating hot mince-pies, telling tales and singing carols.

Suddenly Sam remembered the eyes and he whispered to Brock. 'Someone is watching us. Someone is up on your shelf, Brock.'

Brock looked up and caught the twinkle of the little green eyes behind the holly branch.

'Come out there! I know you. Come out,' he called, and down leapt their old friend from Ireland, the Leprechaun.

'I came to spend Christmas with you,' cried the small fellow, dancing on the table. 'I got a ship from Ireland and I travelled with a tinker to the Christmas Fair. I crept in here, and hid on the shelf, and I was going to appear on

Christmas morning, but your family spied me, Brock. You're not angry, are you, Brock? You are glad?'

'You are very welcome!' cried Brock. 'Father Christmas told me he had seen you. He said you'd maybe call to see us. I'm glad indeed you're here to share our fun.'

The Otters were excited to talk to the Leprechaun, of whom they had heard from Sam Pig. They said they too would stay for the night, and sleep on the floor.

Ann clapped her hands when the Leprechaun made white roses blossom on the holly boughs, and nightingales sing in her work-basket. 'It's just like old times,' she said, remembering the days after haymaking that the Leprechaun had spent with them.

'I'll make a tiny bed in the corner for you,' she told the wee man.

'I've got the heather mattress you used to sleep on,' said Sam. 'And the pillow of wild thyme, and the blanket of wool from the black sheep,' added Tom.

'We'll feed you on honeycomb and heather ale, and mince-pies and green herb cheese, and Christmas cake, and plum pudding,' said Bill.

The little Leprechaun was happy as a sandpiper, and he sat down and cobbled his shoe with a bit of bat's wing leather Brock provided.

'I must get it ready to hang up for Father Christmas,' said he. He and Brock had much to tell each other, for each was a person of great age and wisdom and knowledge of magic.

There was a gentle tap on the door, and at first nobody heard it, for everyone was laughing and talking and admiring the Leprechaun's work. The Otters were singing, the pigs were chattering, and still the tap went on.

'There's somebody else tapping besides me,' said the Leprechaun. 'Who is it?'

Sam opened the door a crack and looked out. The Lady Echo stood there, in her white dress, covered with snow, and her gold hair lit up with snow-stars.

'Come in, Lady Echo,' invited Sam.

'Come in, Lady Echo,' answered the Echo, and she floated into the room, like a drift of snow. Her eyes sparkled like the stars, and a scarf blue as the sky lay on her shoulders. She was glad to be in the homely room, instead of out in the wide fields alone.

'Have you come to spend Christmas with us?' asked Sam.

'Come to spend Christmas with us,' replied the Echo, and she dropped a chaplet of snow-flowers on the table and brought a little Christmas tree from the folds of her gown.

She was scarcely seated, when there was a little shrill whinny at the door, and a stamp of tiny hooves.

'Father Christmas is here,' said Sam, dashing forward to throw open the door. Nobody entered, but a flurry of snow-flakes fell, smothering the floor in white. Lady Echo drew her dress close to her, the Leprechaun stopped mending his shoes, and Brock took the pipe from his mouth.

'Who's there?' he asked.

Nobody answered, but again the sharp high whinny rang through the air, and in the whiteness of the snow they could just distinguish a silvery shape, like a slim little horse, standing outside.

'Oh, it's my Unicorn!' cried Sam, flinging open the door. And there was the Unicorn, wearing a silver crown on his head and with a wreath of snow dangling from his horn.

'Come in, Unicorn,' called Brock, but the Unicorn refused.

'I will stand here near your door,' said he. 'I want a word with the eight reindeer when they come with Father Christmas.'

'But you'll be so cold,' said Sam, holding out his hand.

'No, I'm in my element. I love the snow and ice,' said the little Unicorn, and he went back to the blue shadows of the snow-covered trees and waited there.

Again there was a tap at the door and this time it was a loud rap-rap-rap, which startled Sam.

'Who's that?' he called. 'Who is it?'

'It's Joe Scarecrow,' replied a high windy voice.

'Go on, Sam, open the door,' called Brock. 'It's one of your friends, tell Joe Scarecrow he is welcome.'

On the doorstep stood the man of straw and wood, with his battered hat on his head, his wooden arms outstretched and his one leg stamping in the cold.

'Please, Master Brock,' said the scarecrow. 'I've come to wish you a Happy Christmas and many of them. When it comes, that is.'

'Come in, Joe Scarecrow,' called Brock, and the scarecrow hopped into the room and stood against the wall.

'Welcome, Joe,' said Sam.

'Spend Christmas Eve with us, Joe,' said Brock. 'We are having a party tonight. Stay the night here.'

'Thank you, Master Brock, I don't mind if I do,' said Joe. 'It's main cold and sharp out in that ploughfield. Nips your fingers, it does. Usually I'm taken into the barn for the winter, but Master Greensleeves has forgot me this time. I'd be glad of a bit of comfort and a sight of Christmas cheer.'

He looked round and bowed to Lady Echo, and stared at the Leprechaun, and nodded and smiled at the rest of the company.

'You've got some grand folk here tonight. It's a bit of a do, like,' said Joe, amiably, and he removed his hat and put it on the floor.

Sam brought some sandwiches to his friend of the ploughland, and Brock gave him a mug of heather ale and Ann fetched the largest mince-pie from the oven.

'Thank ye kindly,' said Joe Scarecrow, pulling his forelock of straw, and holding up his mug to drink their healths.

Then Sam got out his fiddle, and they all sang, 'Here's a Health unto His Majesty' and 'Peace on Earth'.

The little pigs were yawning, the Otters were blinking their round eyes, Lady Echo was singing to herself, 'Peace. Peace. Peace on Earth.' Brock said it was time everyone went to bed.

Suddenly Lady Echo began to sing in a clear, high voice a carol she had heard long ago, and kept in her memory. The words floated in the air, and Sam listened dreamily. Then he crept softly upstairs to bed, and he hung up his hat on the bedpost. Tom, Bill and Ann followed their brother. The little Otters curled under the table and softly snored. The Leprechaun climbed into his own tiny heather bed in the corner and hung up his shoe. Joe Scarecrow took off a ragged sock and held it out. Then he shut his eyes and fell fast asleep, standing as usual on one leg.

Brock the Badger went to the door and looked out. The Unicorn stood there, as if made of ice, under the bright stars and the motionless trees. The lovely song of Lady Echo came from the room, thin and high and unearthly, bringing its memories of a Christmas long ago.

Brock waited, leaning on the doorpost, watching the sky. Suddenly he saw Father Christmas riding there on his sleigh with the eight reindeer jingling tiny bells. Down over the tree-tops came the sparkling hoofs, down to the ground. The sleigh rocked with the load of toys, and Father Christmas climbed out, waving a hand to Brock the Badger.

'Are they all ready? Are they asleep?' he asked, in a voice soft as the fall of snow.

'Yes, they are all ready,' answered Brock. 'All except Lady Echo. She is remembering past days.'

The Unicorn awoke and stepped daintily up to the team of reindeer. He nuzzled against them

and talked to them in his own language, of Iceland and Greenland and Fairyland.

'I shall go with you,' said he. 'I shall travel to that land near the moon. I am ready to go tonight.'

Father Christmas was unpacking his sleigh to find presents for the company in Brock's house. He carried odd little parcels down the chimney and dropped them in the hats, the pockets, the fur pouches of the Otters, the ragged sock of Joe Scarecrow and the tiny shoe of the Leprechaun.

He drank a mug of honey-mead with Brock and stayed by the fire, with Lady Echo singing softly, and the little Otters snoring.

'A Happy Christmas, Brock, old fellow,' said he.

'Same to you, Father Christmas,' replied Brock.

'Take care of them, Brock,' said Father Christmas.

'Yes, I'll guard them from harm,' replied Brock.

Then Father Christmas said good night, and left his blessings on the little house. He climbed into the sleigh and gathered up the reins. He chirruped to the eight reindeer and was about to drive off when he noticed that a small silver horse was in front: a horse with a slender horn growing from its forehead and with a silver crown on its head.

'A Unicorn!' cried Father Christmas. 'Now that is a surprise. I wonder where he has come from.'

'Oh, I know him well,' said Brock who was standing in the doorway to watch his old friend's departure. 'We call him "Sam's Unicorn". He has been waiting all this night to join you.'

'Well, I'm glad to have him, for my reindeer want extra help with the great load they have to carry now there are so many little children in the world.'

He chirruped again, and the Unicorn tossed his

head and the cavalcade moved away. Up into the air it swept, high over the tree-tops, across the blue night sky, among the stars.

'Bless you,' said Brock, and he went indoors and sat down in his big chair to sleep, but Lady Echo still sang her gentle carol: 'Peace. Peace. Peace on Earth.'

The next day Sam sprang from his bed and looked in his hat. It was bulging strangely, and he brought out a pair of bone skates.

'Happy Christmas, everybody,' he called, and all the rest awoke and felt in their hats, their socks, their purses, and their pockets.

Tom found a cookery book, and Bill found some toffee apples. Little Ann had a pair of fur mittens, and the Leprechaun found a *History of Merlin the Magician* tucked in his shoe. The little Otters had marbles made of moonstones and opals in their pockets to play with on the sandy river-bed. Joe the Scarecrow found a muffler and a stick of his favourite Blackpool rock. Lady Echo had a gleaming necklace, made of snow-pearls, and Brock the Badger felt in his furry pocket and brought out a telescope to look at the sky.

'The loveliest presents ever known in Brock the Badger's house,' cried Sam, and he ran out-of-doors to discover the marks of the reindeers' hooves and the imprints of the runners of the sleigh. The hoof marks were clear in the smooth snow, with the little Unicorn's dainty prints.

On the snow lay a little silver circle, the crown

the Unicorn had worn. It had fallen off when he rose into the sky with Father Christmas.

Sam took it to Brock, who hung it on the Christmas Tree.

They stood round and held hands, and sang the Christmas Day hymn for all things, great and small, men and children and animals.

'A Happy Christmas, World. A Happy Christmas, World,' they cried, and their small voices flew out over the hills to the stars, while down on earth the church bells rang their merry peal.

The Weather Cock

At the top of the steeple of the parish church stood a Cock. For many years he had balanced himself on the slender spire, twisting and turning with the wind, gazing over the wide countryside. From where he perched he could see green meadows and the shining river, thatched cottages half-hidden by clustering sycamore trees, the village school with its clanging bell, and the busy little street.

There was always something going on down below, and as the Cock's eyes never closed, he saw more than most people.

He watched the ploughman guide his horses across the fields in the early spring, when the gulls wheeled around his head, screaming their news as they searched for food. He saw the reaping machine gather the corn in autumn, when the pheasants rose with a clatter of fear. He watched the fisherman cast his line into the swirling waters of the river, and draw out the slim silver fish.

He saw the babies brought to church in long white robes, and years later marry, and bring their own little children. He heard the chatter of voices in the playground, and the drone from the school, which lay next to the church. No one could say the Weather Cock's life was dull. He even looked into the nests of the rooks, and had a word with the cawing birds, who hurried home to their young ones.

'Hurry up, hurry up,' he cried. 'Young Jack is leaning over the edge of the nest. A little farther and he will fall and break his neck.'

'Hurry up, hurry up,' he called again in his rusty creaking voice. 'A thief is stealing the sticks from your nest.'

The rooks flapped hastily by, cawing their thanks.

When the East Wind blew he warned the old villagers to stay indoors and sit in the chimney corners.

> East Wind, East Wind,
> Stay behind, stay
> behind,

he sang.

Of course he pronounced Wind in the old way, for he had been there for close on two hundred years.

And when the wind blew from the North he flapped his iron wings and called:

> A Wind from the North,
> Pray don't come forth,

and everybody shut and bolted the doors and fastened the shutters, as the gale howled round the cottages and threatened to take off the roofs.

When the wind blew from the West, he called:

> A West Wind, a West Wind,
> Put on your cloak and never mind,

and the old people put their cloaks and coats on their backs, and walked down the street to see what was a-doing.

But when the wind blew from the South, he gently cried,

> A Wind from the South
> Is sweet to the mouth,

and the aged men and women came out of their cottage doors to sit in their little gardens, and young children brought out their bread and milk to eat under the sycamore trees.

It was a great responsibility, keeping all the very old and very young from harm, besides warning the farmer, and helping the birds, and the Weather Cock at last got tired. He often felt lonely, too, as he watched the long-tailed bright-eyed cock in the poultry yard at the farm strut up and down, with proudly lifted feet and fine long spurs. How he envied him!

He wished he, too, could pick up grains of corn from the cobbled yard, and scratch among the straw. He longed to fly on to the open half-door of the barn and shout 'Cock-a-doodle-doo' to the brown speckled hens gathered below, gazing at him in admiration.

One winter's night he stood brooding on the steeple, listening to the singing of hymns in the church below. It was Christmas time, and the choir boys were practising. The Cock knew every hymn by heart, he had heard them so often during his two hundred years of life. But this time all was different, he felt lonely and sad, and a strange pain came in his breast.

A tear dropped from his eye, and then another and another. But the icy North Wind blew on them, the frost froze them, and they dropped in the churchyard below as little balls of ice.

'It's hailing!' cried the little choir boys as they scampered, with red and blue mufflers round their necks and pink buttons of noses peeping out, down the church walk to their homes.

The Cock wept for loneliness, and the hailstones bounced down on the path below. Whatever was the matter with him? He had never felt like this before! He had never been able to cry. It was a new experience, and the tears rolled down faster.

The hours chimed from the clock in the steeple, and still the Cock wept. Midnight fell, and a shiver went through the iron breast of the Weather Cock.

His feet felt suddenly light, his wings moved with ease. He stretched them out, drew himself up to his full height, and flew out into the night.

Down, down, he flew from the high steeple, past the churchyard with the white graves, and the ivy-covered school, past the smithy and the miller's house, to the farm-yard. He nestled under the haystack and fell asleep, for the first time in his life.

In the morning he joined the flock of hens and the black-tailed cock.

They showed him the warm hen-house with its little narrow staircase, down which they climbed each morning when the farmer opened their door, and they took him to the water trough where the icy spring flowed.

The villagers stared up at the empty steeple in amazement. They rubbed their eyes and fetched their spy-glasses, but the Cock had completely disappeared. Only the big letters, N, E, W, S, were left. So they asked the blacksmith to make an angel to stand on the steeple, and tell them about the weather.

But when the farmer saw the new Cock with his iron-grey feathers and his fine red wattles, he said to his wife:

'Here's a splendid bird, come to bring Good Luck to us on Christmas morning; for it's my belief he's flown down from yonder steeple.'

'It's the right place for an angel,' said the Cock to the crowd of sympathetic hens. 'He can take care of the village, but as for me, the barn door is my steeple,' and he flew up to the open door, and cried, 'Cock-a-doodle-doo'.

The Three Wise Men

One Christmas Eve, during a heavy snowstorm, a man and his young wife sat talking by the fire. They lived in a lonely little cottage beyond the village, and there were many days when they saw nobody. That did not prevent the wife from being merry and cheerful, but the husband often wished for company.

'Last year we went to Cousin Goodman's for Christmas Eve, but we can't go anywhere tonight,' he grumbled. 'Hark to the gale out there! How wild it is!'

The wind howled like a wolf and the trees howled back. The door latch rattled, as if somebody were touching it. The snow swept up in drifts across the garden, and piled itself high against the walls.

'It's a bad storm. Nobody could go out on a wild blustery night like this,' agreed the wife. 'I'm thankful we have a good roof over our heads, Simon.'

'Aye. We've a lot to be thankful for, I suppose,' Simon answered gloomily. Mary threw a fresh log on the fire, so that the flames danced in the chimney and showers of sparks made a little fountain like the fireworks on Guy Fawkes's day. It was a cheerful sight, she thought, to see the yellow flames and the gold caves in the fire. She fetched some apples from the larder and put them in a tin in the oven by the fireside to bake for supper. She spread the blue and white cloth on the table, and brought out the Sunday plates and mugs.

'It's Christmas Eve, and a feast night,' said she. 'We always have our best china on this night.'

There was cream from their own cow, Strawberry, next door in the little cowplace. Mary set it on the table in the old silver jug. Even as she paused to polish the jug, she could hear the rattle of the chain and the thud of the cow's body against the dividing wall. She put some milk on the fire to warm for the Christmas Eve posset, and added cloves and a dash of ale to it for her husband.

'Now I'll make our Christmas Eve posset. You'll like that, won't you?' she said. She lifted down the posset mug from the mantelpiece while her husband watched her. There was a candle burning on the mantelpiece, shining out over the little room, and as it was Christmas Eve she lighted another and placed it in its polished brass candlestick on the table.

'Aren't we grand tonight?' she laughed. 'We might be expecting company, so fine we are.

When I was little, it was Santa Claus himself who came round on this night, and weren't we excited! I do love Christmas Eve.'

She smoothed her hair in front of the little glass on the wall, and she put on a clean linen apron and her mother's gold brooch. 'There,' she said, 'now I'm ready for the king himself.'

Her husband only stared at the fire. His young wife was always making little jokes, to wheedle a smile to his face. He was anxious and poor and worried about small things.

'It does look nice, Simon, doesn't it?' she asked, kneeling at his side for a moment.

He looked at her sweet face turned to his, and stroked her hair. 'It's lovely, Mary. You've made it grand. I've never seen it so nice before. You can make a feast when there's an empty pantry. You make everything pretty you handle.'

She leaped to her feet with joy at his words, and danced round the room, putting the final touches to the holly and ivy that decked the walls. Along the edge of the stone mantelpiece hung a chain of scarlet berries which she had threaded that afternoon, and in each brass pitcher and pan she stuck a spray of greenery.

There were not many pictures in the little room – a wool-work embroidered picture of Christ blessing the children, a cross-stitch sampler, and a painting of a cart-horse. Round the frames she had twisted garlands of holly and sprays of ivy, and sprigs of berries decked the looking-glass and the dresser.

From the middle of the ceiling hung the Kissing-bunch. It was a large bunch of holly with the choicest berries, all trimmed neatly into a round smooth ball of greenery. It was suspended by a string from a hook, and underneath it a visitor must take a kiss. Such was the custom of those times, when Christmas trees were hardly known.

'It's as lovely a Kissing-bunch as ever I remember,' said Simon, gazing up at it. The ball glittered in the firelight. The rosy apples and yellow oranges hanging in the bunch gleamed, and the silver bells, gilded walnuts and little flags of paper stuck in the Kissing-bunch made a brightness that seemed to shine out like a lamp.

Simon rose to his full height and drawing his little wife close to him he kissed her under the prickly bunch. 'Thank you for making so many pleasures out of nothing,' said he.

At that moment, as they stood there with the Kissing-bunch dangling above their heads, there was a loud thud at the door, and the wind cried more fiercely than ever. They both looked in surprise. The door was locked with the great old key, and bolted with iron bolts, and a mat lay at the bottom to keep the room warm.

'What's that?' asked Mary. 'Is somebody there?'

'Only the wind, my dear,' Simon replied, and pushed the door mat closer.

Again came the thump like a knock on the door.

'Who is it?' asked Mary.

'We'll soon see,' Simon answered, and he drew the bolts and unlocked the door.

Yes, there was somebody there, out in the deep snow. An ancient man stood in the shadows by the cowplace. He didn't speak. He was white with snow, as if he had walked far in it. His back was bowed, but one could see that he was very tall. He leaned on a crooked staff.

'Come in out of the storm,' said Simon. 'What are you doing here at this time of night? Come in, come in, master.'

The old man stepped into the room. He took no notice of Simon and Mary, but he looked round eagerly as if he were seeking somebody. The two stared at him in astonishment. His face was dark-skinned, and wrinkled in a thousand creases, but it had a noble expression, serene and wise. His eyes glittered like stars with emotion as he saw the Kissing-bunch. His clothes were of a strange fashion, worn and old, stained and tattered. On his shoulders was a cloak, white with its covering of snow.

'Who are you, and what do you want?' asked Simon again, but he hesitated as he spoke, for it seemed rude to question such a traveller as this.

'My name is Balthazar, and I am looking for Him,' said the old man, very slowly, and his voice rang through the room like a deep bell.

Mary put her warm young hand on the crooked fingers that clasped the staff, gently released their grasp, and put the staff in the corner.

'Poor old man, you're as cold as ice,' she said. 'Come here and sit by the fire and warm yourself. Make yourself at home, for it's Christmas Eve, and we're glad to have you. There's nobody but just ourselves, so stay the night. We can't turn you out to look for that friend you were talking about. Stay here; bide with us and share our Christmas Eve supper.'

As he turned his intent gaze upon her, Mary was filled with sudden happiness. She poured out warm water for him to wash at the sink. She gave him a towel to dry himself, and she hung up his cloak on the hook behind the door.

'Sit you here,' said she, drawing the Windsor armchair up to the table. 'There's roast apples and mince-pies, and a hot posset to drink.'

She fetched another mug and plate and made ready for him. He murmured his gratitude to her. Before he ate, he folded his hands together, and said a prayer in a foreign tongue. Mary and Simon had their supper with him, waiting on him and serving him, but they did not bother him with questions. When he had finished he sat quietly by the fire.

'You can sleep here, in the kitchen, where it is warm,' said Simon.

'Thank you,' said the old man, 'I shall not sleep, but I shall be glad to wait here for Him. This is a beautiful home.'

Mary smiled happily and nodded at the Kissing-bunch.

'You like my Kissing-bunch?' she said.

'It is a holy thing. This is the kind of place where He might come,' the old man said, simply, and he looked at the bunch of holly as if he could see more than was visible to their eyes.

'Sing your Christmas Eve carol, Mary,' said Simon. 'I am sure our visitor will like it. You always sing it at Christmas!' So Mary, shy before the stranger, sang in a small sweet voice, and Simon played his fiddle to accompany her.

Silent night! Holy night!
All is calm, all is bright;
Round yon Virgin Mother and Child
Holy infant so tender and mild,
Sleep in heavenly peace.
Sleep in heavenly peace.

They said good night and went upstairs, with a backward glance at their strange guest. He sat by the fire, but his head was turned to the Kissing-bunch, and he seemed to be waiting and listening for something.

In the night Mary was wakened by music coming out of the air, filling the whole cottage with exquisite sound. It floated round her and she lay enchanted, listening. It was a high clear tune, like the wind makes, but many flutes seemed to be playing at once.

Sweet and low it went, and then high, ringing through the room.

'Hark! Simon,' she whispered, nudging her husband. 'Listen to that music. Where does it come from?'

Simon sat up. 'It's all round us, Mary,' said he. 'Is it the old man playing something downstairs? Let's go and see.'

'He couldn't play like that, Simon. It's a lot of people playing. Just listen to it.'

They crept softly down the creaking stairs and opened the kitchen door. A golden glow filled the room with radiance and they saw a wonderful sight. There were three men there, and although they recognized the old traveller among them, he was changed. The men were dressed in royal Eastern robes, golden and scarlet and white. They were kneeling on the stone floor with their heads bowed and their arms stretched out holding gifts.

The tall, dark old man, Balthazar, held sweet-smelling myrrh, and the fragrance of it filled the little kitchen. His scarlet cloak, sprinkled with stars, was spread out around him.

Another man, with a long grey beard, held in his hands a lump of gleaming gold. His blue cloak was wrapped closely to him, and his face was hidden.

The third, a young man, had taken off a gold crown which lay near him. His white cloak was like the snow outside. He offered the gift of frankincense, which burned like incense.

The three men knelt towards a light which came from no earthly candle or flame or fire. Under the Kissing-bunch was a heap of yellow straw from the shed next door, and on it lay the Baby. The Child was laughing at the Kissing-bunch and looking up at it. Over Him leaned His Mother, her cloak flowing to the ground, her arms encircling the Holy Child.

The music got louder, voices were now singing, but whether it was really the wind in the bare trees, or angels in the sky, Simon and Mary did not know, for nobody was visible. The music filled the room, the air was sweet-scented and the scarlet berries on the Kissing-bunch gleamed like a thousand candles. The little Child stretched out His fingers towards an apple and a gilded walnut, and He laughed into His Mother's eyes, as she smiled down at Him.

Simon and Mary knelt in the doorway, and even as they looked at the Baby, the light dimmed, and the music became faint. Shadows crept from the corners and the vision faded away. There was only the flickering dying fire which shone on the old man, kneeling under the Kissing-bunch in his dark, soiled clothes.

They closed the door and went upstairs to talk of what they had seen.

'It was the Child Jesus and His Mother and the Three Wise Men,' whispered Mary.

'I remember a tale I heard from my grandmother,' said Simon. 'I had forgotten it till now. There's an old legend that the Three Wise Men every Christmas seek for the Holy Child. They travel from land to land in any Christian country to find the place where He might come, and when they have chosen, they enter, and the Miracle of the first Christmas happens again.'

'Who is the old man downstairs?' asked Mary.

'He is Balthazar, and he goes ahead to find the cottage that is swept and clean all ready for the guests.'

'And the others?' asked Mary. 'Who was that with the crown?'

'That was Caspar, King of Chaldea, and the grey-bearded one Melchior, King of Nubia. But I am very tired, Mary. I feel dazed and strange. My eyes won't stay open and I must sleep.'

Simon dropped on the bed and was fast asleep in a moment, and Mary too was soon lost in dreams.

It was dawn on Christmas Day when they awoke, and at once they went downstairs, hurrying to see the old man, to ask him about the vision. There was no trace of him, not a clot of melting snow on the floor, or a mark of a footstep. Only, hanging in the Kissing-bunch were three little boxes of cedar wood, sweetly perfumed and delicately made. They dangled in the green leaves among the apples and oranges, the gilded walnuts and the silver bells.

'Look!' cried Mary. 'Those were not there last night. Who left them there? Was it the old man – or those others who came?'

'Those others,' said Simon, thoughtfully.

The boxes hung by thin woven grass strings, and he untied the knots and took them down. They were smooth as silk, rare and beautiful, carved from the golden wood. He turned them over, and they flew open to show their treasures. In one was a lump of yellow gold, in another myrrh and in the third an ointment made from frankincense.

'The Three Wise Men have left part of their offering here to remind us of their visit for always,' said Mary.

'We shall never forget this happening,' agreed Simon. 'We will always prepare for the Holy Child on Christmas Eve.'

The next year was a time of prosperity for them, and everything went well. At Christmas a baby had come to share their home and their love. They swept the hearth on Christmas Eve, and hung up the Kissing-bunch, but the Three Wise Men were far away. Their own little child held up his tiny hands to the berries and apples and oranges, and the light seemed to shine down upon him when Mary sang her carol.

Later, when he was old enough to understand, they showed him the three little boxes which the Three Wise Men had brought, and they told him this story of the coming of the Christ Child.

The Fir-Trees and the Christmas Tree

The three pointed fir-trees were sharp against the sky. Their layered branches powdered with white were motionless, and their crests seemed to be up among the stars. At their feet lay deep snow, with never a footprint. The trees stood at the edge of the lawn, where the ground broke away to a precipice. They were the guardians of the old house.

From the house came laughter and the sound of music, for the musical-box was playing a merry tune. Across the lawn the flood of light fell from the unshuttered windows, soft, mellow firelight and candlelight from that home in the hills. The fir-trees stood quietly watching, staring at the room where two children were playing and their mother was setting tea.

They saw the dark shape of a tree similar to themselves, but very very small, on the table; and as they looked at it little lights came on the low branches, and suddenly the tree blazed with candles. Twenty or more coloured candles gleamed like points of gold from the house, and the dark fir-trees across the lawn gazed without a movement of their boughs. Their moon-shadows lay like an intricate blue web on the lawn. Everything was very still.

'What is it, Brother?' asked one of the trees, and it slightly shook its boughs so that a flurry of snow fell.

'It is a Christmas tree,' answered the tallest tree, whose eyes could see twenty miles over the hills and dales. 'It is a little Christmas tree, a baby one.'

'Will it grow up like us?' asked the youngest tree.

The great tree did not answer. It had turned to watch the stars in the sky, for it was Christmas Day and wonders might happen at any moment.

The trees spoke together, they bent lower so that they peered through the window. They had good sight, and they had often looked into that room at the other side of the lawn.

There was the big square room, with thick curtains which had not been drawn over the windows. The shutters which so often shut off the night were left wide open. The trees could see the blazing fire, and the sideboard with the musical-box and lighted candles. They could see the table set for Christmas tea, with all the glitter of silver and best china and the sparkling snowy cake. They had seen the tea-table scores of times on birthdays and Sundays and festivals long before the children or even their parents were born, they were such great trees, but they had never had such an intimate view of a little Christmas tree before.

It stood in the centre of the table, growing in a large green pot, and on its branches were golden balls and silver bells, and little boxes of chocolates and baskets of sweets. There was a silver bird at the top, and a silver house swung from a bough, and stars of silver and icicles hung there.

'Where did that tree come from?' asked the youngest fir-tree. 'Was it always like this?'

'No, it came from the wood by the house,' said the great tree, softly nodding towards the plantation of beech and fir which covered the near hill. 'I saw the Master bring it to the barn, and I thought he had dug up the tree for firewood. I was sorry, for it was a shapely little tree. Now it is decked out like a bride at a wedding. I've seen a few brides too. It's a Christmas tree now.'

'Christmas! Christmas!' murmured the youngest tree. 'I wish I were a Christmas tree on a tea-table.'

'Don't say that,' said the great tree, sharply. 'You could not bear the heat of the fire. You would long for the rain and the wind. We are all Christmas trees, out here on the hillside, with snow at our feet and snow on our boughs.

Besides, we can see the winter sky and the stars and the moon. We can see the angels and the holy spirits of God floating above the clouds. We are happier here.'

'I hope they won't fasten the shutters,' said the youngest tree. 'I could watch that little Christmas tree all night.'

'I think because it is Christmas they may leave the windows free, with no thick curtains drawn across and no wooden shutters,' said the great tree, in a, comforting voice. They watched the sight with great interest – the tea-party, the crackers, the cake with its candles, and they saw the mother and father and children laughing and talking.

'Look. They are all going out of the room,' said the youngest tree. 'Now we can see the Christmas tree more clearly. The candles are burning, the toys are hanging there, and the maid is clearing the tea-things away.'

Down in the valley, far away, the bells of the little village church were ringing joyously that Christmas night. The sound of them came in the clear air like music, as they pealed for evening service. The children and their mother ran upstairs to get ready for the carol-singing. They fetched their prayer books, they put on their thick boots, wrapped themselves in coats and cloaks, lighted a glass-sided lantern, and in a few minutes they came out to the snowy path.

'Look at the Christmas tree through the

window,' said Kate. 'Isn't it beautiful? I like to see it from outside.'

'It's the nicest tree I remember,' said David. 'It is such a good shape this year. Last year we didn't have one, and the year before it had to stand on the floor, and the year before – I can't remember.'

'Our great fir-trees must be surprised to see it,' said Kate, looking across at the three great trees on the lawn's edge. 'I'm glad Mother left the shutters open tonight. Mother, why did you leave the shutters undone?'

Mrs Flowers came hurrying from the door wrapped in her blue cloak with a fur round her neck and a fur muff on her arm.

She, too, looked admiringly at the bright little tree on the table, shining all alone out at the snowy waste of fields and woods and hills.

'I wanted everyone to see it,' said she, simply.

'But there aren't any people up here except ourselves, and nobody ever comes this way,' objected David.

'I wanted the trees and woods and sky and animals to see it. Perhaps a little rabbit will look in while we are at church, or the owls, or – anything. There's Fanny staring at it from across the yard.'

The stable door was open at the top and the mare was peeping at the lighted tree, watching the brightness in the house. She whinnied when the children called and waved their lantern.

'Happy Christmas night, Fanny,' they called. 'You can't go to church. You are safe in your stable.'

'Now, children. You'll be late with all this chattering,' said their father, and he sent them off. Laughing, they all bundled down the steep, snowy lane, with the lantern swinging and their shadows wavering over the slopes. They went through field gates, down the rough pathway between stone walls, and as they went they could hear the merry peal, now near, now far, as they dipped in hollows and walked along ridges.

A lantern bobbed and wavered on the distant hillside, and they knew that a neighbour a mile away was going to church. The lanterns flashed a recognition, the children stumbled and pushed each other, the snow got over their boot-tops, but they only laughed excitedly. The little church at last came in sight. It shone like a lighted ship at the side of the river. Its warm lights were reflected in the running water, and the bells and the sound of the river were mingled together.

People came from the village, from the hamlets, and from the lonely farms, all meeting at the church on Christmas night. There would be carols and Christmas hymns, there would be holly and ivy, and good smells of lavender and paraffin oil and fur and leather. All the scents of Christmas would be there, with flowers from the castle and rosemary from the cottages, decorating the altar and the font.

The church door was wide open, but the red baize inner doors, which kept away the wild winds and the sound of the rushing water, were closed. They pushed, and from the darkness they entered the warm, happy building, so closely packed that they could scarcely squeeze in a pew.

Far away on the hillside the little Christmas tree waited alone in its fairy-like beauty. The farmer came into the room and looked at it with admiration. Slowly he blew out the candles and then he drew the lamp close to his armchair. He opened his Christmas annual and sat down for a quiet read. The fire was enormous, and its blazing logs sent such a glow in the room he could see without the lamp. The heat made him drowsy, for he had been out milking in the cow houses across the fields where the bitter cold came. Now he was close to the fire, utterly content. The man and the maid were out, the children and his wife at church, and he had the house to himself. He shut his eyes and fell asleep.

The fir-trees across the lawn were watching. They saw their Master sleeping there, and they whispered together.

'Be silent,' commanded the great fir-tree. 'Look at the sky. If you see a shooting star on Christmas Day your wish will come true.'

The fir-trees tossed their snow-laden branches and turned their eyes to the sky. They watched the deep-blue heavens which sparkled with a thousand stars. They saw Orion the Hunter and the Great Bear, they saw the lady in Cassiopeia's Chair, and the dancing little Pleiades. As they waited a meteorite came spinning down from the zenith, dropping, dropping in a gold line to the horizon. It seemed the biggest star in the sky as it fell, and each tree made a wish.

'I wish we could have the little tree with us for a few minutes,' said the youngest tree, breathlessly.

'I wish we could wear beautiful lights and toys and bells like the little Christmas tree,' said the second tree.

'I wish . . . I wish . . .' whispered the oldest tree.

'What did you wish?' they asked, looking at their brother, whose topmost bough touched the Great Bear.

'I wished for something not to be told,' said the great tree. 'If we see it, then you will know. That is all.'

'I don't understand what he means,' whispered the youngest tree.

'He is old and wise. He knows many things,' said the other softly.

They all turned towards the gabled stone house across the lawn, for there was a slight movement. The window opened, the candles burst into flame, and the little Christmas tree, with its flags flying and its silver bells tinkling, came floating through.

'It's coming to us. Your wish is coming true,' cried the second tree to the youngest.

The little Christmas tree held out its green skirts like a ballet dancer. Its gold balls were swinging and its silver bird flew. Although it was now out in the cold winter air of that hilly land, the flames burned steadily and the hoar frost sprinkled on the branches was not disturbed.

Like a tree out of fairyland, the beautiful Christmas tree glided across the drive and over the smooth, snow-white lawn to the group of splendid fir-trees on the edge by the rocks. There was a sound of music, for every glass and silver bell rang, and the little glass trumpet fastened to one bough blew and the glass fiddle on another branch played a tune. The needles of the fir rustled sweetly and a delicious perfume came like incense from the tree.

The old mare leaned over the stable door, watching. The dog came from his kennel. The little birds asleep under the eaves of barns and sheds opened their eyes, twittered, and gazed at the sight. Only the Master, asleep by the fire, never stirred.

The glittering little tree rested on the snow under the three fir-trees, and they all looked down on it, so small at their feet. It stayed for a few minutes very faintly singing, with the trees swinging low their boughs to touch it, dropping their snow crystals on its branches. All the candles blazed, the tinsel and bells shone, and a small voice was heard singing praises to God.

Then up rose the tree, and it floated away with its roots trailing behind it, its bells tinkling and its candles burning.

In at the window it flew, only just in time, for as it settled down on the table the Master awoke.

'Goodness me! The window's blown open,' he cried, and he went across the room to shut it.

'That comes of leaving shutters unfastened,' he muttered. 'I'm sure I blew out the candles. I'm sure I did, but I can't have done, yet they don't seem to have burnt away.'

He tucked the tree's roots in the pot and stared very hard.

Then he looked at the grandfather clock, and then at his watch.

'They'll be back from church soon. I'll leave the candles to light them home,' said he.

Out on the lawn the trees were talking. 'What was your wish?' asked the great fir-tree, looking at the second tree.

'That we could be made beautiful as the Christmas tree,' it answered. 'But that can't come true.'

There was a flutter of snow and a shower of hail, and out of the air stepped a sparkling creature, with a bag of snow-crystals on his arm. His snow-feathered feet danced on the lawn, his sleeves dripped with icicles, his face was thin and full of mischief, and his ice-blue eyes were like fire.

'Jack Frost. Jack himself,' said the trees together. 'Jack Frost.'

'I've come to bring your wish,' laughed the great frost spirit, and he danced on the tips of his thin feet, and pirouetted and twisted with dazzling motion like a spinning top. As he swayed he threw handfuls of snow and shining toys over the trees in showers of silver and ice. Snow roses grew on the fir-trees' branches, and iced spangles hung like jewels from every twig. Suns and moons and stars of snow-crystals dangled from the branches with a glitter of beauty not of this earth. Crystals like boxes hung on some branches, and from them spilled wheels and balls and crosses and crowns. Blue and gold, yellow and green, shone the ice as Jack Frost threw the treasures up in the air, high over the crests of the tall trees.

Then the frost spirit fetched Northern Lights out of the air and pinned them to the dark fir trunks. He caught a little star and stuck it on the top of the tallest tree. He plucked a moonbeam and twisted it round the branches, and he threw icy drops from the streams over all the trees so that they were caught and frozen to diamonds.

'Behold your wish,' said he, taking off his plumed hat and bowing. Then he sprang in the air and flew away to sprinkle more toys on fields and woods and window-panes.

The trees stood there, all a-glitter, shining with many colours under the moon, more radiant even than the little tree on the table.

'Oh,' whispered the youngest tree. 'I know I am very beautiful. I wish someone could see me.'

'You have no more wishes,' the great fir-tree reminded it. 'I have mine to come.'

And they all waited in their beauty under the night sky. It was very quiet, they could hear the murmur of the river down in the valley, singing to itself as it strove against the frost, groaning as Jack Frost tried to bind it with his chains. They knew he wouldn't be successful, for the wild little river was never still enough to be caught and imprisoned.

Not a sound came from the farm. The mare had gone to her stall, the dog was asleep in his kennel. The little Christmas tree shone out bravely, and the Master put more logs on the fire and looked again at his watch.

Church was over, and the congregation came out. The families called 'A merry Christmas and a happy New Year!' as they lighted their lanterns and separated for the journeys across the fields and along the lanes to their homes in valleys and on hillsides.

Kate and David and their mother came quickly along the road to their own hills and fields. They could see the lights from the house high up among the stars, and they hastened.

Suddenly little Kate looked at the sky above their heads.

'White birds. See, a flock of great white birds,' said she. 'What can they be?'

A line of snowy birds flew across the sky, and the sound of their wings made music and a light seemed to accompany them.

'They are swans, flying from the lake over the hills,' said David.

'Swans? Are you sure they are swans?' asked their mother, dreamily. 'Swans? Are you sure?'

'Of course, Mother. Of course.'

'I thought I saw . . .' She hesitated. 'They are too far away to be sure.'

The fir-trees also were watching the sky. They also saw the white-winged birds flying across.

'Look at the great birds,' said the youngest tree. 'Why do they fly tonight?'

'They are angels,' said the oldest tree. 'A flight of angels is going across, to see the Christmas trees, to peep at the churches, to see the children, to visit the world. I can see their gold crowns and their hands crossed before them. They are flying to look at the earth. They are visible tonight, the only night of the year.'

The trees bent their heads as the angels flew over. A strong living force was in the air, it passed over the house and around it, it brought peace and happiness with it.

The family trailed up the hill. They saw the fir-trees gleaming with lights and colours in the moonlight, across the shadowy lawn.

'How beautiful they look. The frost has been to them,' said Kate.

'They are as pretty as our little tree,' added their mother. 'I love the fir-trees.'

They went indoors and when they entered the sitting-room they noticed something new. Three little snow-white boxes hung on the Christmas tree, and they had not been there before.

'Where did these come from?' they asked. 'Have you put them there, Father?'

'Nay. I've been to sleep. I woke up and found the window open, though. Somebody maybe came in,' said their father.

They took them down and opened them. In one was a rose of snow, in another a crown of ice, and in the third a cross of crystals.

'Strange things happen on Christmas night if you leave the window unshuttered and let the earth get a good look at your Christmas tree,' said their mother.

She stood at the window and gazed at the three fir-trees. They looked back at her and nodded their heads, and all their toys and flowers and candles were visible, shining with silver and gold. Quietly she pulled the shutters across and drew the curtains.

'Good night, Christmas,' said she.